The Streets Don't Love Nobody 2

Tranay Adams

Lock Down Publications and Ca$h
Presents

The Streets Don't Love Nobody 2

A Novel by *Tranay Adams*

Tranay Adams

Lock Down Publications
P.O. Box 870494
Mesquite, Tx 75187

Visit our website @
www.lockdownpublications.com

Copyright The Streets Don't Love Nobody 2

Lock Down Publications
Like our page on Facebook: Lock Down Publica-
tions @
www.facebook.com/lockdownpublications.ldp
Cover design and layout by: **Dynasty Cover Me**
Book interior design by: **Shawn Walker**
Edited by: **Jasmine Devonish**

Stay Connected with Us!

Text **LOCKDOWN** to 22828 to stay up-to-date with new releases, sneak peaks, contests and more…

Thank you.

Tranay Adams

Chapter One
That night

Cee Cee pulled up inside of the parking lot of The Drunken Monkey. She then looked to Flocka. He was reached between his legs and grabbed one of the two duffle bags. He then reached underneath the seat and grabbed his gun. After popping out the magazine and checking it, he smacked that bitch back in and cocked the slider on it.

Flocka tucked his banga. "Keep her runnin', I'll be back Asap." he hopped out of the Chevy and tucked his banga in the front of his pants. He then slammed the door shut behind him and grabbed up his duffle bag, heading for the back door of the establishment. He pushed open the door and took a quick look around the dimly lit bar. The patrons were drinking, smoking and/or indulging in a game of pool. Everyone seemed to be minding their own business and enjoying themselves.

Flocka looked over to the bar and spotted the same bartender he'd seen when he and Menace first came in to holla at Raffy. Flocka ambled over to the bar where he ordered up a Heineken and requested to see Raffy. The bartender nodded and walked to the end of the bar, where he snatched a green beer bottle. Turning around, he grabbed a bottle-cap opener and popped the lid on the Heineken. He stopped before Flocka and sat the Heineken in front of him on top of a napkin. Flocka thanked him and dropped a blue face Benjamin Franklin on the bar top.

"That's all you, my boy," Flocka took the beer to the head, throat rolling up and down as he guzzled its contents.

"'Preciate it," the bartender told him as he stuffed the bill inside of his pocket. He then walked over to the telephone, which was hanging on the wall. He pressed a single button and listened to the telephone as it rung. On the third ring, someone picked up his call. He swapped words with whomever it was for a second. He placed his hand over the receiving end of the telephone and looked over his shoulder, addressing Flocka, "My friend, what is your name?"

"Flocka," Flocka called out to him over the loud ass music.

Flocka watched as the bartender gave him his back again and chopped it up with whomever was on the telephone for a second. Right after, he was hanging up the jack and telling him to head up to Raffy's office.

"My man," Flocka tapped his fist against his chest and walked towards his destination. He climbed the staircase and knocked on Raffy's office door. A moment later, he heard a buzzing sound and then the door was clicked unlock. Flocka opened the door and made his way inside of homeboy's office. Once again, he saw Raffy sitting behind his desk, talking to someone over his Blu-tooth. His legs were crossed and he was squeezing a small royal blue ball, looking like he was really into the conversation he was having. Flocka whistled for his attention. Raffy glanced up at him and held up a finger, signaling for him to give him one minute to wrap up the conversation at hand.

"Got cha, thanks again," Raffy disconnected the call and set his sights on Flocka. His eyes then fell down to the duffle bag that the young gangsta was holding at his side. "My friend, is that my money in that bag?"

"It sure the fuck is. I threw in interest too, since I'ma lil' late," Flocka walked over to Raffy's desk and dropped the duffle bag in front of him. He then sat down in the chair that was positioned before his desk.

Raffy sat up in his chair and pointed at the duffle bag, saying, "That's my money? Every last red cent of it?" he asked like he couldn't believe the young nigga was dropping a bag on him. He'd already made up his mind to smoke his ass because he felt in his heart that he wasn't going to come up with the money to pay his debt. He had to put his foot in his mouth now though, homeboy had showed up with his due.

"Like I told you the first time, homie, that's you and then some," Flocka stated proudly. "Go ahead and count that shit up, 'cause I ain't leavin' out this bitch, 'til I'm sure we square. I don't want no blowback from this. You Griff me?"

"Right," Raffy took off his Blu-tooth and sat it on his desk top. He then pulled out his calculator and a money counting machine. Next, he pulled the duffle bag closer to him and unzipped it. When he peered inside of the duffle bag, he saw several bankrolls with rubber bands wrapped around them. Raffy licked his lips and rubbed his hands together, greedily. He couldn't wait to run through those bands to see exactly what he was working with.

Flocka sat back in his chair and took the half smoked blunt he had tucked behind his ear. He held it up to Raffy's line of vision, asking if he could smoke in his office. Raffy gave him the nod, and he pulled out his Bic lighter. He stuck the blunt in between his lips and produced a blue flame, firing it up. Flocka sucked on the end of the blunt and blew out smoke into the air. Taking the occasionally pull from the blunt; he watched Raffy count up the money he'd given him.

Raffy finished counting up all of the loot and tossed it back into the duffle bag. He then he pulled open his desk's bottom drawer and placed the items he'd use to count the money with inside of it. Next, he removed the portrait from the wall behind his desk, revealing a safe. He did the combination to the safe and opened it. He took out of all of Flocka's jewelry and passed it to him, watching him put the jewels back on. While Flocka was busy putting his jewelry back on, Raffy was stacking the money from duffle bag inside of the safe. Once he shut the door, he laid back in his chair looking at Flocka and grinning. "You know, normally I don't care how I get my money just as long as I get it. But due to these circumstances, I have to ask out of curiosity, how did you manage to get your hands on all of this cash in such a short time?" Raffy inquired as he clipped the tip of a Cuban cigar and pulled out a lighter designed like a jukebox to light it. Holding the flame of his lighter to the tip of his cigar, he sucked on the end of it, and waited for Flocka to answer him.

Flocka smirked and said, "I made a few moves, called a couple of markers in. As it turned out, I hadda couple more dollas than I needed once thangs came together."

Raffy blew out a cloud of smoke and sat the jukebox lighter down on his desk top. He knew Flocka was full of shit, but he wasn't going to press his line for the real story. He was just happy to get what was owed to him without having to spill blood. "And there you have it, huh?" A smile spread across his lips.

"And there you have it," Flocka smiled back at him, lifting his hands from off the arm rests of the chair and then dropping them.

There was silence between the two men as they stared at one another. Flocka finally stood to his feet, and decided to break the silence. "Listen, I gotta get goin'. I got some more moves I needa make, so I'll get up witchu whenever. We good?"

Raffy nodded as he sucked on the end of his cigar. He blew out smoke before responding, "Yeah, we're good."

"That's what's up," Flocka outstretched his hand to shake Raffy's hand, but he didn't budge to oblige him. The mothafucka just looked at his hand as if it he'd just pissed and didn't bother to wash it. "Come on, my nigga, don't leave me hangin'."

Still smiling, the Arab shook his head. "I'm sorry, but I'm a germaphobe."

Flocka frowned and dropped his hand at his side. "Whatever, Blood, I'm outta here." he turned around and made a beeline toward the door, his walk slightly off thanks to his fake leg. Raffy frowned when he saw the difference in his walk, but didn't mention it. He contributed it to the real reason behind him being able to pay him his debt.

****

Once Flocka had gotten back outside, he switched seats with Cee Cee and drove her to her house. When he pulled up outside of her house, he put his Chevrolet in *park* and looked at her house, through the windshield. He then set his sights on her. Lightning fast, he drew his gun and pressed it to the side of Cee Cee's head, bending her dome to the side. Fear ceased her eyes and she lifted her

11

hands in the air again. Her eyes were staring out of their corners. Her heart thudded and her palms grew sweaty. At that moment she wondered whether homeboy was going to kill her or not.

"I thought you said you weren't going to kill me," a fearful Cee Cee asked.

"And I'm not, consider this a warnin'," Flocka began. "If you mention anything about how we set up that lick, or where I just dropped that bag off to, yo' ass is done for. I'm pullin' back up to yo' house and I'm knockin' every-body's head off. I don't give a mad ass fuck who up in there. You hear me?"

"Yes, I hear you. I'm not going to say a word to any-one, no matter what," Cee Cee swore teary eyed.

"Good. Now, get the fuck outta my ride!" he took the banga from her temple and sat it on his lap. He watched as she hopped out of his car, slamming the door shut behind her and making hurried steps toward her house. Flocka waited until she was inside before he put his Impala in *drive* and drove off.

Later that night

Flocka and LaRon were sitting on the couch playing Madden and sharing a blunt. They blew out smoke from their nose and mouth, as they continued to play the game. The smoke inhabiting the living room made it look like they were inside of a sauna.

"Yeah, nigga, I'm getting all up in that ass!" LaRon talked that shit to his sibling. He was twenty-one points up on his older brother.

"Whatever, mothafucka," Flocka waved him off and took a couple more puffs of the bleezy. His face was swollen from Menace pistol whipping him, but it was beginning to go down. "The game just getting started. I still can come back and chip you, fool."

"Bet something, then," LaRon challenged him.

Flocka looked at him like he was crazy, twisting his face up. "Bet these nuts!"

Boom!

The door swung open from a powerful force and splinters scattered everywhere. Menace and Fonzell, who were masked up, rushed inside with tranquilizer guns. Their handguns were tucked at the front of their pants. They pointed their tranquilizer guns at Flocka and LaRon, just as the twins were grabbing their bangaz from off the coffee table. LaRon grabbed his gun first. He whipped around to fire, but Menace shot him in the neck with a dart which was tainted by a sedative.

"Gaaaah!" LaRon winced and dropped his gun. He clutched the dart in his neck and pulled it out. Looking at the dart with blurring vision, he realized he was about to fall asleep. Before he knew it, his eyes rolled into the back of his head and he dropped to his knees. As LaRon fell flat on his face, LaRon pointed his gun at Menace, about to knock his head off.

Bocka! Bocka!Bocka!

Fonzell pushed his son out of the way just in time for the gun bursts to miss him. Pissed off that LaRon had tried to take his son's life, Fonzell dove to the floor and scooted his back up against the couch. He sat his tranquilizer gun aside and whipped out his banga.

"Nigga, you gon' try to murder my boy? I'll kill you, mothafucka!" Fonzell swore angrily.

"Pop, no, I want 'em alive!" Menace called out to his father from where he was inside of the kitchen. He'd crawled there once his old man had shoved him out of the way of the gunfire.

"Fuck this nigga, junior!" Fonzell called back out to his son.

"Alive, pop, alive!" Menace shot back.

"Ain't nobody killing me, both ya'll niggaz dead! That's on everything I love!" Flocka swore. He kept his gun pointed as he kneeled down, placing two fingers to LaRon's neck. Having confirmed that his brother had a pulse, Flocka picked up his gun. "Neither one of you cocksuckaz are leaving outta this bitch alive!"

Flocka looked from left to right, pointing one gun at the end of the couch that Fonzell was taking cover behind, and the other in the direction of the kitchen. He scowled and clenched his jaws, before banging his guns at both locations.

Bocka! Splocka! Splocka! Bocka! Bocka! Splocka! Bocka!

Bullets whizzed through the opposite end of the couch, knocking the stuffing out of it. The other bullets flew through the wall of the kitchen, tearing big ass holes in it.

Fonzell scrunched up his face and turned his head, narrowly missing the slugs coming through his end of the couch. He gripped his gun and clenched his jaws, heatedly. Fonzell was one second from coming from behind the couch and knocking Flocka's head off his shoulders.

"Junior, you got about ten second before I lay this son of a bitch down, you hear me?" Fonzell called out to his son from where he was taking cover.

"Bitch nigga, you ain't laying shit down, eat slugs!" Flocka's face twisted with mortal hatred, and he sent some more heat Fonzell's way.

Splocka! Splocka! Splocka! Splocka!

Bullet's shredded one of the couch's fluffy pillows and knocked more stuffing out of the end that Fonzell was taking cover at.

"You hear me, boy?" Fonzell called out to Menace again.

Meanwhile, Menace searched the cupboards until he found a bag of flour. Crouching back down to the floor, he made his way back over to the end of the kitchen. Poking his head out of the kitchen's doorway, Menace locked eyes with his father and showed him the bag of flour. The young nigga communicated through eye contact the plan he had in mind, and they exchanged nods. Afterwards, Menace disappeared inside of the kitchen, waiting for his time to strike.

Menace counted down to three and sprung to his feet. He called out LaRon's name and launched the bag of flour in his direction. Flocka's head snapped in the direction that Menace was at and he fired a shot at him. The bag of flour burst and sent flour everywhere, leaving the surrounding areas cloudy. Some of the flour splattered in Flocka's face and temporarily blinded him. Still holding his guns, he bitched and complained, trying to wipe the flour from out of his eyes.

When Menace saw that Flocka was distracted, he fired a dart at him. The dart stuck to his chest like a refrigerator magnet, causing him to grunt in pain. Right after, Fonzell came up from where he was taking cover beside the couch and fired a second dart into LaRon's neck. Having been hit with the second dart, Flocka fired blindly at Menace and Fonzell. Menace and Fonzell ducked out of the way of the flying bullets. A second later, Flocka's arms dropped to his sides and he released his guns. His eyes rolled to their whites and he fell toward the floor, banging his head on the edge of the coffee table.

"Come on, son," Fonzell motioned Menace out of the kitchen with his tranquilizer gun. "Let's get these fucks bound and shipped outta here. I know the cops are on their way, with all of that gunfire, thanks to this piece of shit!" he kicked Flocka in the head, slightly lifting it off the carpet. He then tucked the tranquilizer gun at the small of his back and whipped out his gun.

Menace walked into the living room where his father was standing. He sat his tranquilizer gun down on the couch and whipped out a roll of gray duct tape. He went about the task of taping up Flocka's and LaRon's wrists while his father held them at gunpoint.

"It's been a minute. I'ma go check on lil' momma," Fonzell told his son.

"I'm good, pop!" Shatira called out.

Menace and Fonzell looked to the staircase. They found a masked up Shatira escorting Delores down the stairs at gunpoint. Delores was bleeding at the side of her head and her hands were held up in the air. She looked like a prisoner of war as she descended the staircase.

"Check my boo out, she held it down," Menace smiled and ran over to Shatira. Still holding her gun, she threw her arms around her man's neck and they stared into one another's eyes, kissing lovingly.

"You proud of me, babes?" Shatira asked.

"Hell yeah, you handled yo' business, slim." Menace took Shatira's gun from her and walked over to Delores, clocking her at the back of the head. The older woman hit the carpet out cold, snoring aloud. After passing his lady her gun back, Menace gagged and restrained Delores wrists behind her back.

Menace rose to his feet after restraining Delores and said, "Alright, crew, let's get these mothafuckaz in the trunk of the car."

Police car sirens blared in the distance as the threesome went about the task of loading Delores and the twins into the trunk of the transporting vehicle.

****

Menace pulled up into the woods and killed the engine. He and Shatira hopped out of his car and made their way to the rear of it. Stopping at the back of the car, he pulled out his gun and motioned for Shatira to stand aside. Once she obliged him, he popped the trunk and lifted it up. Inside were the twins, Levon and LaRon, gagged and restrained. Menace pointed his gun at LaRon. The bitch ass nigga squeezed his eyelids shut and bit down on his bottom lip, turning his face for fear of being shot in it.

"Get out! Get cho punk ass outta the trunk!" Menace commanded, but homeboy didn't budge. Angry, he flipped the gun over so that he'd be holding the barrel of it in his hand. He then leaned over inside of the trunk and started whacking LaRon's punk ass upside the head with it. When he drew his hand back, the handle of his banga was stained burgundy. He took the gun by the handle and pointed it back at his dome piece. "Get out, mothafucka, I'm not gon' tell yo' ass not one mo' time!"

LaRon squeezed his left eye shut so that the blood running from his forehead wouldn't get into it. Using nothing but his legs, he climbed out of the trunk of the car. He missed his step and fell face first onto the ground, dirtying his face. As he winced, Menace grabbed him under his arm. "Come on, get cho ass up! Get up on yo' feet!" he pulled him up to his feet and walked him over to where he wanted him to be, forcing him down to his knees at gunpoint. "Stay here! You move, and I'll gun you down, you hear me?" LaRon didn't answer. He bowed his head and his body trembled. Hot teardrops fell from his eyes and splashed on the surface. "I said, 'did you hear me, nigga?'" he pressed the gun to his forehead and lifted his head up, forcing his sorrowful eyes to meet his unforgiving eyes. At that moment, LaRon looked pitiful as fuck. He didn't look anything like the hardcore thug he'd proudly portrayed himself to be.

"Mmmmmhmmmm!" LaRon tried to say something, but the duct tape muffled his voice.

"Youza pussy, Blood, you ain't got no heart, 'less it's somebody weaker than you that chu facing. I don't respect that shit! Matter of fact, I don't respect you!" Menace lowered his gun and kicked LaRon in the head hard as fuck. The mothafucka slammed into the ground, wincing. Then, he slowly pulled himself up from the surface, looking dizzy and shit. "Babe, bring that other bitch ass nigga over here!" Menace motioned for Shatira to bring Flocka, the oldest twin over to him with his gun.

It was a struggle, but Shatira was able to get Flocka out of the trunk. He took three steps before his legs gave out on him and he fell to the ground. This was due to his legs falling asleep during the long drive over to the woods. Shatira went to help him up, but Menace calling out to her stalled her.

"Don't help that nigga up, move out the way, baby!" Menace said to her, pointing his gun down at Levon's knees. As soon as Shatira moved out of the way, he fired a shot that sent dirt up into the air. Flocka turned his head just in time to miss the bullet, he then got to his feet in a hurry.

Levon forced the duct tape from off his mouth with his tongue and said, "What kinda game you playin', nigga, huh? If you gon' kill us, then fuckin' kill us!"

"Bitch, shut up and dance!" Menace growled and clapped at Levon's feet, making him dance around as clouds of dirt sprayed up into the air. Once he stopped firing, the oldest twin stood where he was breathing hard, chest jumping up and down. The shooting at his feet left his heart thudding hard. "Hahahahahahahahahaha! And they say gangstaz don't dance." Menace smirked for a second then focused his attention back on Levon's punk ass. "Get cho ass over here witcho bitch made ass brotha, Blood, and hurry up!" Levon started making his way over to his brother, but he wasn't moving fast enough for Menace. Angry, the young nigga smacked him across the back of his skull with his gun, dropping him down to one knee. When he tried to get up, the young nigga kicked him in his ass and he crashed to the ground, sliding the side of his face in the dirt. Lying where he was he took a breath, and blew a small dirt cloud into the air. Menace stood behind him, pointing his gun at the back of his head, hostility written across his face. "My nigga, get up and get over there 'fore I split cho wig!"

It took some effort, but Levon got upon his feet. He walked over to where his brother was on his knees and got down on his knees beside him.

Menace stood before the twins looking between them. LaRon was weeping like a little bitch and begging for his life. Levon was mad dogging him and vowing to kill him, as soon as he was given the chance.

"You gon' kill me, huh?" Menace asked Levon with a smirk. He found the oldest twins threats humorous, given the fact he was in a losing situation.

"You can count on it, mothafucka!" Levon lowered his head and glared up at him. The boy had the look of the devil in his eyes. Having grown tired of his mouth, Menace pressed the tape back down over his lips

"Pardon me, boo," Shatira tapped Menace on his shoulder and he stepped aside. She stood in full view of the twins clutching a shovel, her hateful eyes staring down at them. "Y'all remember me?" When the twins looked at her like they didn't know who the fuck she was, Shatira pulled the bandana down from the lower half of her face to reveal her identity. The twins appeared to be shocked, then. "Yeah, y'all remember me, so I know you also remember how you were gonna rape my ass that night, right?"

Levon shrugged his shoulders nonchalantly. This pissed Shatira off royally. She cocked back the shovel and swung it at his dome with all her might.

Cliiiiiiing!

Levon's head snapped to the right and he fell backwards on his back. Shatira stepped over him and cracked his ass a couple of more times, before she stepped to his younger brother. She kicked him in the head hard as shit, knocking him down on his side. She then hit him in every exposed part of his body, causing him to wince more and more with each blow.

Shatira drew the shovel back over her head in an attempt to strike LaRon's ass again, but bright blinding lights stopped her in her tracks. She and Menace looked up to see who it was approaching, and met the headlights of a Tahoe truck. She lowered the shovel at her side and gazed at it, placing her hand above her brows.

"Relax, babe, that's pop." Menace informed her, watching the Tahoe as it neared them and circled around them.

The Tahoe stopped and Fonzell jumped out, slamming the door shut behind him. He made his way around the back of the SUV and opened the hatch. Reaching inside, he grabbed a gagged and restrained Delores under her arm, pulling her along.

"Now that mommy's here, we got ourselves a family reunion." Menace smiled devilishly

Menace and Shatira had their backs to the twins, leaving them vulnerable. Making a mental note of this, Levon alerted LaRon and nodded his head to them. Using the sway of his head, he showed LaRon who to attack so they could try to make a run for it. LaRon nodded in agreement of the plan, and they stood up on their bending knees. They exchanged knowing glances, and that's when all hell broke loose.

Levon lowered his head and ran forward, tackling Menace. The collision knocked Menace's gun out of his hand and he crashed to the ground. Levon then took off running past his brother. By the time Shatira whipped around with the shovel, LaRon was tackling her to the ground. LaRon almost crashed to the ground with her, but he caught himself. He then went to run after his brother but thunder erupted.

Blowl

The back of LaRon's head exploded and he crashed to the surface. A furious Fonzell, who had kicked Delores to the ground seconds before, walked up on him. He extended his gun at his back and emptied the clip at it.

Blowl! Blowl! Blowl!Blowl! Blowl! Blowl!

Looking up from where she was lying on the ground, Shatira saw Delores running off into the opposite direction. Determined to stop that bitch's escape, Shatira searched the ground for Menace's gun. Locating it, she picked it up and sprung to her feet. Murder danced in her eyes as she chased after her stepmother.

"Tonight's judgment night, bitch!" Shatira snarled, with her gun extended at Delores back as she ran.

Blocka! Blocka!

Delores shoulders danced as she caught hot shit in her back and crashed to the ground.

Shatira casually walked up on that bitch. She kicked her in the side and demanded she turn over on her back. Slowly, Delores turned over on her back, wincing from her gunshot wounds.

"I guess this is it, huh?" Delores asked as she coughed up blood.

"You mothafucking right." Shatira mad dogged her, keeping her gun pointed down at her face.

"Well, here's a little secret I've been carrying, I killed your father," she told her with no remorse. A smile slowly spread across her face, and then she started laughing manically. "Hahahahahahahahahahahahaha!" Delores' laughing agitated Shatira and she emptied her clip in her face.

Blocka! Blocka! Blocka! Blocka! Blocka! Blocka!

"Tell me something I don't know, punk ass ho!" Shatira lowered her smoking gun and tucked it at the small of her back. She then grabbed a dead Delores by her ankles and drug her back in the direction that she'd come from.

<u>Chapter Two</u>

Menace got upon his feet just as the gunfire rang aloud. He looked over his shoulder in the direction that Shatira had ran, and then back at his father, who was blazing at Levon as he fled. At first, he didn't know whose aid he should come to. But after hearing the report of his own gun several more times, he figured Shatira had finished off Delores, and he should go help his father. Having made up his mind, Menace chased down his father. He'd gotten halfway into the woods to find Fonzell trying to reload his gun. Fonzell had tucked his gun under his arm and went to pull out the extra magazine from out of his pocket. Moving too fast, he fucked around and dropped the magazine to the ground. Seeing that Levon was getting away, Menace snatched up his father's magazine and took his gun from him. Fast and expertly, he smacked the magazine into the bottom of the handgun and cocked that shit back. He then chased Levon a short way through the woods, watching him zig zag between trees. Menace pointed his gun and cracked off three shots, missing Levon. Gripping his gun with both hands and aiming it carefully, he pulled the trigger. The bullet ripped through the air. Levon's head snapped to the right and blood sprayed from the side of his dome. He crashed to the ground shortly thereafter. Having seen him go down, Menace tucked his gun and recovered Levon's dead body. He dragged his kill back into the direction that he came from

****

Menace and Shatira met back up with the dead bodies of Levon and Delores. As soon as their eyes met, they ran towards one another relieved. Colliding, they wrapped themselves in one another's arms and kissing. Holding her at arm's length, Menace looked her over for any wounds and she did the same. Coming to the conclusion that they both were okay, Menace and Shatira looked to Fonzell.

He looked okay, but Menace still wanted to check on his old man. He approached him with his gun extended at its handle's end. His old man took the gun and tucked it on his waistline. He and his son then hugged.

"You good, pop?" Menace asked, generally concerned about his father's wellbeing.

"I'm straight, but I could use a pick me up, though." Fonzell shamelessly admitted, referring to him needing a shot of dope.

"Well, these mothafuckaz graves are already dug, me, lil' momma and Ducey can bury 'em while you get right." Menace told him as he grabbed the other shovel from out of the ground. It had been standing straight up in a pile of dirt, beside a grave.

"Nah," Fonzell shook his head, "I'm not gon' get high in front of yo' girl."

"Pop, she been known that you do what chu do. Ain't no shame in the shit. It is what it is."

"You're right." Fonzell patted his son on the cheek.

Menace knocked on the hatch of the window of the Tahoe and Ducey stuck his head out of the driver's window. "Yo', unc, can you give us a hand?"

"Sho' thing." Ducey hopped out of the truck and followed Menace so they could bury the dead bodies.

Fonzell watched as Ducey, Menace and Shatira attended to the corpses for a while. Afterwards, he climbed back into the front passenger seat and slammed the door shut. Reaching underneath the seat, he pulled out his worn black leather case which had everything in it he needed to cook up dope. Once he had the belt pulled tight around his arm, he administered the shot of heroin. Afterwards, he pulled the syringe out of his vein and removed his belt, sitting it beside him on the seat. His eyes became hooded as the heroin took its effects on him, he found himself nodding on and off. The average person looking at him would have thought he was just dozing off to sleep, but someone from the gutta would be able to tell he was a dope fiend well under the influence. Shortly thereafter, a fog rolled over Fonzell's brain, and he recalled an event from his past once again.

Fonzell sat on his bed Indian Style playing his guitar and freestyling a song off the top of his head. He had an ink pen behind his ear and a notepad lying on the bed before his eyes. While playing the instrument and singing, he'd occasionally stop to write down the lyrics he liked.

Fonzell was crooning lyrics as he played his guitar when he heard a knock at the door. When he glanced at the clock on his nightstand, it was after midnight so he wondered who it could have been at his home at that hour. His curiosity had gotten the best of him so he decided to see exactly who it was at his door. With that in mind, he took the ink pen from behind his ear and leaned his guitar up against the wall. He hopped up out of the bed and made his way down the hallway, making a beeline toward the front door. He peered through the curtains. After identifying who it was on his porch, he unchained and unlocked the door. As soon as he pulled the door open, he was taken aback by the presence of Moochie. Her individual braids hung loosely around her face, but Fonzell could see the black and blue bruising on her cheek. On top of that, she had a busted lip and her right eye was swollen shut.

Seeing tears rolling down Moochie's cheeks, Fonzell took her by the hand and walked her inside of the house. He then stuck his head outside of the door, looking up and down the street for anyone who may have followed her to his home. Once he saw that the coast was clear, Fonzell shut the door and locked it back. He then focused his attention on Moochie, leading her over to the couch and sitting down beside her.

"What happened?" Fonzell asked concerned, sweeping the loose braids from out of her face and tucking them behind her ear.

"He..-he found out about us," Moochie reported, wiping away her tears with her fingers.

"Your husband?" his brows furrowed and his heart thudded.

"Yeah," she nodded.

"Fuck!" he ran his hands down his face, exhaling. He looked stressed as a mothafucka now. Homeboy was familiar with how her husband got down, so he knew he'd be met with his wrath when he found out he was fucking around with his wife. "How'd he find out?"

"I was playing with myself in the bathtub and I called out your name," she admitted. "He busted open the bathroom door, yanked me outta of the tub by my braids and shoved a gun inside of my mouth. He asked me were we fucking around, and if I lied he'd blow the back of my head out." she sniffled and wiped her dripping eyes again.

"Hold on, limmie get chu something," Fonzell left out of the living room and returned with a few Kleenexes. He sat back down and handed them to Moochie. He rubbed her back soothingly and watched her blow and wipe her nose. "Go on, finish telling me the story."

"I told him what was up with you and I and he pistol whipped me," she told him. "He pointed his gun at me and was about to shoot me, until I bit him on his ankle. As soon as he went to grab his ankle, I kneed him in the nuts and grabbed some clothes. I didn't even have time to get dressed inside. I heard him coming, so I jumped out of our master bedroom's window. I ran away slipping this dress over my head," she looked down at the flower printed dress and tugged lightly on the fabric. "I hitch hiked a ride to your house, and here I am."

Moochie broke down crying and Fonzell embraced her. He kissed her on the side of her face and rubbed her back, lovingly. She cried her eyes out on his shirt, and he encouraged her to let it all out. Once she'd finished weeping, Fonzell held her at arm's length, looking into her eyes.

"Oh, shit, we've gotta get the fuck outta here?" Fonzell said wide eyed, looking fearful.

"Why? What's the matter?" Moochie asked curiously.

"Nine times outta ten, he's on his way over here. We've gotta get the fuck outta here, asap."

Fonzell hopped up from the couch. He was about to run off when Moochie called after him.

"Yeah?" Fonzell looked over his shoulder, forehead deepening with lines.

Moochie looked nervous to tell him what was on her mind as she fidgeted with her fingers. Swallowing the lump of fear in her throat, she looked back up into the man's eyes she truly loved.

"I'm pregnant," she spat it out, watching for his reaction.

"Are you sure?"

She nodded and said, "Yeah. I'm two months. I went to the doctor's appointment two days ago. I would have told you sooner, but that's quite a big bomb to drop on someone."

Fonzell nodded his understanding. He then ran his hand down his face and massaged his chin. "Is it mine?"

Moochie looked Fonzell in his eyes. Right then, he knew exactly who the father of the baby was growing inside of her belly. When she broke down sobbing, he rushed over to her and hugged her, lovingly. He consoled her as she sobbed long and hard, caressing her back.

"Shhhhhhh," Fonzell tried to hush her sobbing, as he continued to caress her back. "Everything is going to be alright. I got us."

Moochie peeled her face up from Fonzell's shirt and looked up at him, tears streaming down her face. "You really mean that?"

"Yeah," Fonzell nodded, looking down at her. "Listen, we've gotta get the hell from outta here. This place is gonna be crawling with old boy's goons any second now."

"Okay. But where are we gonna go?"

"There's a cabin up in the mountains. It belongs to my old man. I haven't been up there in a year, but we should be safe there."

"Alright."

Fonzell kissed Moochie on the forehead. He then packed a few things and grabbed his guitar. Once he *came into the living room, he peered out of the curtains to make sure there wasn't anyone outside waiting on them. Once he was sure there wasn't anyone lurking in the shadows to knock him and his girl off, he unlocked the door and headed out to his car.*

Yo', Fonzell! Fonzell!" Ducey called out to his running partner. He was turned around in the driver seat, leaning over into the backseat and shaking Fonzell hard so he could wake his ass up.

Fonzell blinked his eyelids repeatedly, beginning to come out of his dope fiend lean. Once he was coherent, he looked at Ducey to see what the reason behind him calling his name was.

"Yeah, what's up, Ducey?" Fonzell asked with hooded eyes, leaning his head back and scratching underneath his chin.

"Put that shit up, man. It's time for us to roll out." Ducey told him.

Fonzell looked up from where he was in the front seat, and saw the car Menace and Shatira had rolled in before him. His son was looking at him. He had one hand on the steering wheel while his arm hung out of the driver's window.

"You good, pop?" Menace asked concerned.

"Yeah, I'm good, son." Fonzell replied as he started storing the items back inside of the black leather case.

"We outta here, OG, I'ma get up witchu later." Menace told his father.

"Okay, junior. I love you." Fonzell told his boy as he pulled open the front passenger door.

"I love you, too." Menace threw up two fingers and drove off.

Right after, Ducey drove away from the woods. Unbeknownst to them, as the red brake lights of their vehicle disappeared into the night, one of the piles of dirt from the graves they'd dug began to move.

****

Flocka stirred awake hearing banging at his apartment door. He searched for his prosthetic leg and found it leaned up against the nightstand. The banging continued at the door as he grabbed it and put it on. He grabbed his gun from underneath his pillow and got up to answer the door, wondering who the fuck it was that had the nerve to disrespect his shit.

Flocka signed once he glanced through the peephole and saw who it was. He didn't know what the mothafuckaz wanted that were on his doorstep, but he sure as hell wasn't up for any bullshit. Flocka unchained and unlocked the door. He then pulled it open, coming face to face with Bumpy's short ass and the goons he'd dropped by the hospital with. They all wore hard faces and looked like they were ready to fuck his ass up.

"'Bout time, nigga, you ain't hear my ass knockin' at the doe?" Bumpy spat with attitude. Eyebrows slanted and face scrunched up.

"Man, I was sleep." Flocka frowned up, wiping the scum out of the corner of his eye.

"Well, yo' ass is up now, so throw on somethin' so we can go."

"Go where?" his forehead crinkled.

"To find the dicksuckas that have boss dawg's money. Now, the man gave you twenty-four hours," Bumpy held up his Rolex watch and tapped his finger against the face of it. "I trust you made good on the promise you made,

30

and have a lead on that paypa, 'cause if not, yo' skinny po' black ass is gettin' fitted with cement shoes and tossed over into the gotdamn ocean."

Flocka's eyebrows arched and his nose scrunched up. He clenched his jaws and clutched his banga so tight his knuckles bulge. "Are you threatenin' me while I gotta gun in my hand, mothafucka?"

"Yes, I am, 'cause I know yo' hoe ass ain't got the balls to use it," Bumpy told him confidently. "And even if you do raise that piece of shit nine, the niggaz with me will have already pulled out and dropped yo' bitch ass in this livin' room. Now, like I said, throw on somethin' so we can go find this money." he harped up phlegm and spat on the carpet, keeping his daring eyes on Flocka the entire time.

Flocka was hot as a mothafucka. The vein at his temple throbbed angrily. He was clenching his teeth so hard his head started shaking a little. He'd never had a nigga totally disrespect his gangsta before. No one had ever had the balls to violate him. And even if they did, he would have blown their mothafucking head off. Standing right there before Bumpy and his homeboys, Flocka knew he didn't stand a chance against them. He was outnumbered and outgunned. The only outcome from that confrontation would be him lying in a pool of his own blood.

Coming to the conclusion that the odds were against him, Flocka decided to fall back.

"My nigga, what the fuck you waitin' for? Go! Hurry the fuck up! Come on, come on, come on," Bumpy clapped his hands harder and harder, each time he said 'Come on'. He then pointed toward the master bedroom.

Flocka shut his eyelids briefly and took a deep breath, to calm himself down. Having calmed down some, he headed back into his bedroom to throw on a shirt, vowing to kill Bumpy's punk ass one day.

Two minutes flat, Flocka marched back into the living room, sliding his arms inside of his jacket. As he neared the door, Bumpy tossed a ski-mask to him and he grabbed it. He glanced at it and stuffed it inside of his back pocket. When that little gangsta ass nigga tossed him the mask, he knew they were going to wind up catching a couple of bodies that night.

Flocka left out of his apartment pulling the door closed behind him. As he headed outside along with Bumpy and the goons, he tried to think of a plan that would spare him Big Meat's wrath.

Fuck, this bitch ass nigga Bumpy and his goons are expectin' money and blood tonight. And if a nigga doesn't deliver, then that's gon' be my ass. I gotta think of somethin' quick. I mean, real quick.

"Come on, man, hop yo' ass in," Bumpy said from the front passenger seat. He and the the goons were inside of a van, idling at the curb. Flocka was so wrapped up in his thoughts that he hadn't even noticed that everyone had already gotten into the whip.

Flocka ran over to the van and hopped inside, sliding the door shut behind him. As the driver pulled off, he lay back in the seat, trying to formulate a plan that could get his ass out of hot water.

"Alright, homeboy, what spot we hittin' up first about this bag?" Bumpy looked over his shoulder into the backseat at Flocka. The van they were in had just pulled up to a red stop light.

This shit gon' be foul, but fuck it! I rather it be them than me, Flocka thought to himself. He then gave Bumpy the address of the person he believed had the money from the pickups.

"Cold world! Now, who woulda thought that cho folks had that bag this entire time?" Bumpy shook his head. "I tell you, you can't trust a damn soul these days."

***

Cee Cee was standing at the kitchen sink washing dishes and rinsing them off, sitting them inside of the dish rack once she was done with them. Twenty minutes ago, her parents and little brother had retired to their bedroom, leaving her to clear the table and clean up the kitchen. This was Cee Cee's regular chores and she didn't mind doing them. Hell, she'd become accustomed to them some time ago.

Cee Cee finished the last of the dishes and dried her hands off. She then pulled the drawstrings on the garbage bag, tied them up and pulled the bag from out of the trashcan. Holding the bag at her side, she headed for the front door, singing the lyrics to one of SZA's songs.

Boom!

The front door flew open and splinters shot across the living room. A frightened Cee Cee dropped the garbage bag and backpedaled from the door. Flocka speed walked into the house with Bumpy and the goons on his heels. His face was a mask of anger and the mothafuckaz with him looked like they wouldn't hesitate to pop a nigga.

"Flocka, what's goin' on? Why'd you kick in my-" Cee Cee was cut short once she saw Flocka whipped out his banga. Her eyelids stretched wide open and she gasped. She was about to run, but he popped one in her stomach. Cee Cee howled in agony and grabbed her stomach. She looked at her bloody hands and then back up at Flocka, like she couldn't believe he'd shot her. Right after, she collapsed to the floor, lying there wincing with a mouth full of blood. Seeing Flocka approaching with his smoking gun caused her to fear for her life. She turned over on her stomach and started crawling toward the front door.

"Fuck you think you goin', hoe?" Flocka came around to the front of Cee Cee and mashed his sneaker against her hand. She hollered out as she felt her knuckles being crushed beneath his foot. Flocka pulled her up off the floor by her hair and forced her up against the kitchen counter. "Where's the money, huh? Where's the money you stole from Big Meat?" he asked loud enough for Bumpy and the goons to hear him. He had to put on a show to make it sound and look good.

Cee Cee looked at him bug eyed and confused, saying, "What-what are you talking about? I don't know anything about no...gaaag." She gagged as he wrapped his gloved hand around her neck and applied pressure. She placed her hands on top of his hand trying to get him to loosen his grip, but from the fire in his eyes she knew that he wasn't going to show her any mercy.

"Don't chu lie to me, bitch! I swear 'fore God I'll pop yo' ass. You hear me?" Flocka's hateful eyes bored into hers as he clenched his jaws and caused them to throb.

"You see what chu can get outta that bitch, we'll search the rest of the house," Bumpy told Flocka. He then motioned for the goons to follow him with his gun, marching toward the back of the house.

"Fa sho'," Flocka said as he continued to stare into Cee Cee's terrified eyes. At this time, her eyes had welled up with tears that threatened to run down her cheeks. There were veins covering her temples and forehead that looked like they were going to explode under the pressure of Flocka's iron-clad grip.

"Why-why are you doing this?" Cee Cee managed to say, trying desperately to pry his fingers from around her throat.

Flocka looked around to make sure that Big Meat's men weren't around. Seeing their shadows cast on the walls from the different rooms that they were inside, he went on to address Cee Cee in a hushed tone, "This shit foul, but a nigga gotta do what he gotta do."

"Bitch, where the fuck is that money at, huh? Where the fuck is that money?" Flocka heard Bumpy barking at whom he assumed was Cee Cee's mother.

"I swear to God I don't know, I don't know about any money!" Cee Cee's mother screamed hysterically.

"Please, leave my mommy alone!" Cee Cee's little brother called out angrily.

"Ah, fuck! This lil' fucka bit me!" one of the goons hollered out.

Smack!

A small body fell to the floor after being back handed

"Fuck it y'all! Ain't no money in this bitch, splash the whole mothafuckin' family!" Bumpy ordered the goons.

Boc! Boc! Boc! Splocka! Splocka! Poc! Poc! Poc! Poc!

Realizing that he had to act now, Flocka released Cee Cee and she hunched over. She held her stomach wound as she coughed, struggling to breathe again. While she was doing this, Flocka tucked his banga on his waistline and snatched a butcher's knife from out of the knife block. Having made sure that the other men weren't approaching; he slashed himself across the arm and tossed the bloody knife at Cee Cee's feet.

"Aaaah! You dirty fuckin' bitch!" Flocka's face balled up and he pulled out his gun. As soon as he did, Cee Cee looked up at him with a pair of horrified eyes. She went to plead for her life, but it was already too late.

Blocka! Blocka! Blocka!

Once Cee Cee dropped to the floor dead, Flocka lowered his banga at his side. His shadow loomed over her as he observed his handiwork. He didn't bother looking over his shoulder as he heard four pair of shoes entering the room from behind him. He stood where he was breathing hard from the make believe struggle he'd put up.

"Fuck, man, what happened?" one of the goons asked curiously.

"Bitch, cut me, man, she was 'bouta try to make a run for it so I cut her ass down."

"Damn, G, she got chu good," the other goon grabbed him by his wounded arm and saw the blood sliding down his fist, dripping on the floor. Quickly, he snatched one of the small decoration towels from off the door handle of the stove and tied it around his arm to stop the bleeding.

"Fuck, we ain't gon' neva get Big Meat's money now," the other goon complained

"Oh, yes, we will," Flocka insured him as he tightened the towel around his arm using his teeth.

"How? Nigga, you done smoked the bitch! Dead hoes don't talk!" Bumpy chimed in.

"I got the name of the nigga that was in on the lick with her. He's the one holdin' the bag. All we gotta do is track this mothafucka down and get it." Flocka informed him.

"Then who? Who has boss dawg's money?" Bumpy asked.

Flocka looked to Bumpy and the goons that ran up in Cee Cee's spot with him. He ran his hand down his face and took a deep breath. He acted like what he knew was stressing him out.

"Come on now, nigga, spit that shit out." Bumpy urged him.

Flocka massaged the bridge of his nose and shook his head. Looking back up at Bumpy and the goons, he said, "Menace."

"Yo', that's yo' man, so I know you know where homie lay his head at, right?" Bumpy asked from the front passenger seat of the van.

"Yeah, I know where live at." Flocka confirmed.

"Good, 'cause we headed over there, right now. Gemmie the address, youngsta."

Flocka gave Bumpy Menace's address. He then directed his attention out of the back window, watching the streets whip past him in a hurry. He couldn't help feeling like the biggest piece of shit in the world for what he was about to do to his brother from another, but looked at his actions as a necessary evil.

"Are you sure it's Menace that has boss dawg's money?" Bumpy asked.

"Yeah, I'm fuckin' sure. The bitch told me before I offed her ass." Flocka told him.

"If homeboy got that loot, then that doesn't make you look so good."

"Fuck you mean, Blood? That was that nigga, I'm my own man." He looked him up and down, scowling.

"Get the fuck outta my face 'fore I leave yo' faggot ass bleeding beside this bitch." A frowning Bumpy nodded to a deceased Cee Cee. She was lying on the floor with bug eyes and an opened mouth, blood pooling beneath her lifeless body.

Flocka took a step back from out of Bumpy's face, but kept mad dogging his ass. "You needa watch cho mouth."

"I'm not watching shit, nigga. I'm telling you cold hard facts." he looked him up and down with disgust. "Menace having that bag ain't gone look right to boss dawg. Him being yo' right-hand man gone make it look like you and him were in cahoots to steal his dough."

"How in the fuck is it gone look like that?" his forehead creased. "In case any of you mothafuckaz haven't been paying attention, I lost my fucking leg during that lick! Why in the fuck would I set up a gotdamn caper where I lose a limb? I'd think I'd be smarter than that, dickhead!"

"I would hope so, but plans don't always go the way we want 'em to, sweetheart." he gave him the evil eye. "As far as my black ass is concerned, yo' punk ass is still a suspect, until proven otherwise."

"Whatever mothafucka! This isn't the time, or the place to be goin' back and forth witcho ass. I'm sure you can hear those sirens, so you know The Boys are on the way. I don't know about chu, but I'm not tryna stick around to find out how much time we'd be lookin' at for four fuckin' bodies. I'm outta here." Flocka bumped his way past Bumpy, making his way toward the door talking shit about Bumpy's ass all of the way.

<u>Chapter Three</u>

There were three piles of dirt deep in the heart of the woods, covered by scattered leaves and twigs. Something within the third pile of dirt began to move. It wasn't long before fingers emerged from out of the ground. One hand came into view, and then another. Shortly thereafter, a man rose out of the ground, wide eyed and gasping for air like he'd come up from out of water. The dirt slid off of him easily, but a lot of it clung to him. He shook the dirt from off of him and stood erect, brushing the remnants off his clothing. He looked to the other two piles of dirt, seeing that they were shallow graves.

"Ma, LaRon!" It dawned on Levon that his mother and younger brother were probably buried in the graves. He dropped down to his knees and used his hands to claw out the dirt, tossing the ground at his back. He found himself growing hot, sweaty and tired, but he ignored what he was feeling. His sole focus was getting his loved one from out of the ground.

"Whichever one of you is in here, hold on! I'm digging as fast as I can!" Levon said, digging faster and faster. Slowly, he began to see someone's facial features. He kept at his digging, and the facial features filled out until he was able to see exactly who the face belonged to. It was his mother, Delores' face. And from her expression he could tell that she was dead. Instantly, Levon's eyes were stung by hot tears. He whimpered and stopped digging up the dirt. Still down on his knees, his shoulders slumped and he dropped his head. He started sobbing, and his head bobbed. Big teardrops fell from his eyes and splashed on the dirt.

Levon brushed the dirt from out of the creases and crevasses of Delores' face. He kissed her on her forehead and pressed his forehead against her forehead. He squeezed his eyelids shut and more tears bursts through his eyes.

"I'm sorry, ma. I'm truly, truly sorry." he kissed her forehead again. "I'ma get chu outta here once I dig up, bro."

Levon crawled over to the last grave and dug as fast as he could. Sweat dripped from his brow. He found himself getting exhausted. His heart pounded madly, but he continued his digging of the ground. The more he dug, the more of his brother became visible. His sibling's limp hand seemed to magically appear before his eyes. Abruptly, Levon stopped digging and dropped his arms at his side. His chest heaved up and down, as he stared down at his brother's grave. The tears in his eyes built up and spilled over, soaking his cheeks. He knew his brother was dead.

Levon fell on his back and stared up at the sky. His tears continued to cascade down his face as his nostrils flared. He found himself balling dirt into his hands and making them into fists. His eyebrows slanted and wrinkles formed between his eyes. His jaws clenched so hard that the muscles in them pulsated intensely.

"I'm gonna get even, I'm gonna get those mothafuckaz, all of 'em! I promise, bro. Niggaz is gon' answer for you and ma's death in blood, tubs of it!" Levon released the dirt from his palms and got to his feet. He looked to his mother's and his brother's graves, crossing himself in the sign of the holy crucifix. Right after, he began his long trek from out of the woods, grabbing a branch to protect himself along the way, just in case he ran into any threatening creatures in the night.

They're dead! Every last one of those cocksucking mothafuckaz. I swear on my momma's and baby bro's graves, Levon thought as he walked through the woods, keeping his eyes open for anything that opposed his life.

****

When Levon had finally made it from out of the woods, he found himself at a highway divider. He casted the long branch he'd acquired on his trek aside, and watched the automobiles as they flew up and down the highway. Once Levon felt like the oncoming automobiles were at a safe distance for him to cross, he ran over to the other side of the highway. Having made it to the other side, he leaned over with his hands on his knees breathing heavily. He wiped the sweat from off his forehead with the back of his hand, and then stood upright. Before his eyes he saw a gas station with a telephone booth on the side of it. Telephone booths were thought to have grown extinct long ago, but apparently this was one of the last standing ones.

Levon hopped over the divider and made his way down the slope, nearly falling. He crossed a second road and walked across the gas station's parking lot. He snatched up the telephone and pressed it to his ear, dialing 9-1-1. Once the operator answered, he told her where she could find the bodies of his mother and brother.

"I'd like to report three more bodies, too," Levon told the operator, then looked over both of his shoulders, listening to the operator. "Yeah, three of 'em. Their names are Menace, Shatira and Fonzell. You'll find 'em

41

somewhere in South Central, Los Angeles reallllll bloody."

Levon dropped the telephone, letting it rock back and forth as the operator continued talking.

"Hello? Are you there? Sir, are you still there? Hello?" the operator went on and on.

****

Levon crept to the end of a building and looked around its corner. He spotted a hood ass nigga stop outside the entrance of a liquor store on his Beach Cruiser and lay it down on the pavement, before heading into the store, pulling a few dollars out of his sagging pants pocket. Once homeboy had disappeared through the entrance, Levon came from around the corner. Hunched down, he looked around sneakily to see if anyone was watching him. Seeing that the coast was clear, he crept over to the Beach Cruiser stealthily and picked it up. He then turned it around in the direction that its owner had rode it from. He hastily walked the bike until it picked up his desired speed. Once it did, Levon hopped on the triangle shaped cushion seat and pedaled down the sidewalk.

"What the fuck?" a voice came from Levon's rear as he pedaled. He looked over his shoulder and saw the hood ass nigga that owned the bike. He had a Swisher sweet tucked behind his ear and a bottle of something stuffed in a brown paper bag. "Aye, nigga, that's my shit! Gimmie my mothafuckin' bike back, cuz!" Homeboy dropped the brown paper bag and it exploded on the sidewalk. The contents of the bottle soiled the bag a darker brown. The hood ass nigga ran as fast as he could, trying to catch up to Levon. The wind blew against him, knocking off Dodgers fitted cap and the Swisher he'd tucked behind his ear. His plaid blue shirt ruffled and showcased the wife beater he wore underneath it. "You bitch ass nigga, if I catch you I'ma kill you!" homeboy swore, trying to close the distance between him and Levon.

When Levon glanced over his shoulder and saw that hood ass nigga was still on his ass, he stood up off the cushion on the Beach Cruiser, pedaling faster. Levon pedaled as quickly as he could, and before he knew it, homeboy was far behind. He glanced over his shoulder again, and dude was slowing down to stop. Shortly thereafter, he stopped in his tracks, hunching over and placing his hands on his bending knees. He breathed huskily, occasionally glancing up at Levon, as he was quickly becoming a dot before his eyes.

"Fuck, cuz, I gotta lay off the Newports." the hood ass nigga said, angrily. He then stood up and kicked an out of order telephone booth; walking off into the direction he'd lost his fitted cap and Swisher.

****

Once Levon had lost old boy, he coasted the rest of the way home on the Beach Cruiser. Instead of going through the front door of his house, he decided to take the alley. He did this in case Fonzell and Menace were at the house. The last thing he wanted was them to spot him and put a cap in his ass before he had a chance to put a couple in their asses.

Once Levon made it behind his house inside of the alley, he put the kickstand down on the Beach Cruiser and krept over to the gate. He leaped upon the gate and pulled himself over. He jumped down and landed on his bending knees. Once he rose, he looked over at Fonzell's house and saw a light on in the bathroom.

Glad dem mothafuckaz home, 'cause I'm finna smoke the whole house. That's on my dead granny, Levon thought to himself as he walked up the backdoor steps and peeled back the mat. He snatched the small copper key that was lying beneath it and opened the door. He stepped inside of the house and pulled the door shut behind him. Next, he ran into the living room and made his way up the staircase. Once he reached the landing, he went straight into the bathroom, where he looked himself over in the medicine cabinet's mirror. He was covered in dirt from head to toe, and his eyes were red webbed. Turning his head, he spotted a deep bloody gash on the side of his head, that had left some of his cornrows partially burgundy.

"Sssssss!" Levon winced in pain as he dabbed his fingertips against the gash on the side of his head. He looked to his finger tips and found them bloody. He then leaned forward and turned his gash to the mirror, studying it carefully. Seeing that the wound was deep enough for him to need stitches, he dipped low to the floor and opened the bathroom sink's cabinet. He removed the yellow First-Aid kit and sat it on the sink, opening it. He took the time to clean his wound, applied some A & D ointment and stitched it up, wincing as he handled the task. Once he was done, he abandoned his filthy clothing on the bathroom floor and turned on the shower water. He adjusted the dials to a temperature of water he was comfortable with before stepping inside of the tub. The bathroom slowly manifested a fog, creating a home made sauna.

Levon placed his hands on the tiled wall and bowed his head. He allowed the hot water to beat off of him, feeling like one-thousand thumbs tapping against his body. The water washed all the dirt and grime from off his form, sending it swirling down into the drain. He got soapy and washed off again. Next, he took out his corn-rows and shampooed his hair, washing the chemical from out of it. After shutting the water off, Levon snatched a towel off the rack and dried himself off. He wrapped the towel around his waist and stood before the medicine cabinet's mirror. He threw four cornrows into his hair and retreated to his bedroom.

Levon got dressed in a hurry. He threw on a tank top, camouflage cargo pants and combat boots. He then strapped on a Kevlar bulletproof vest and threw a duster on over it. Next, he flipped over his mattress and grabbed the AK-47 he'd stashed underneath it. He loaded that bitch up and grabbed the extra banana clips he had on deck, stuffing them inside of his duster's pocket. After-wards, he cut out all of the lights upstairs and made his way down stairs. He walked inside of the kitchen and peered out through the curtains hanging over the window. He smiled wickedly when he saw the bathroom light was still on next door at Fonzell's house.

****

Levon came out of the back door of his house and shut the door back, quietly. He snuck down the steps and tip toed over to the dividing fence. He tossed his AK over into the backyard and then he hopped the fence, landing on his bending knees. He looked around. Seeing that there wasn't a soul around watching him, he snatched up his AK and made his way up the steps. He placed his ear to the back door to listen in. His wicked smile stretched across his face again when he heard voices coming from the other side of the door.

"Yeeeah, I'ma 'bouta get all ya asses." Levon said to no one in particular. He then stepped back from the door and kicked it in with all of his might. That bitch flew open, sending splinters flying. Levon braced the stock of the AK-47 against his shoulder and ran inside, slightly hunched over. He went through the kitchen, to the living room, pointing the deadly end of his choppa around, ready to catch a body. Once he'd cleared the first floor, he crept up the steps as quietly as he could. The closer he neared the landing the louder the talking became to him.

Levon, with the AK-47 held low, moved down the hallway sneakily, making his way towards the bedroom with the voices coming from it that he'd heard downstairs. Having reached the door where the voices were clearly coming from, Levon hoisted up his AK. He took a step back from the door, took a deep breath and then kicked it open. As soon as the door flew inward, he rushed in, AK up ready to fire. He lowered his AK once he saw there wasn't anyone inside of the bedroom. Turning around, he saw a home video playing on the flat-screen. It was a birthday party for Moochie and Fonzell. Fonzell was wearing a party hat and singing *You're just too good to be true* to her as she cried happily.

Blatatatatatat!

An angry Levon blasted on the television and sent sparks and fire flying everywhere. He then pulled the TV to the floor as he left the bedroom, causing it to make a loud crashing sound as he cleared the threshold.

****

"This it?" Bumpy asked as he looked up at Menace's house.

"Yeah, this the place." Flocka confirmed, looking at the house himself.

Bumpy looked at the goon behind the wheel and said, "Park this mothafucka so we can go see about this pay-pa."

The goon obliged the little gangsta's orders.

"Okay," Bumpy started back up as he reloaded his gun and cocked it back. "Me and Flocka will take the front doe, and y'all two niggaz take the back doe. Is that okay with every mothafucka in here?" No one opposed his orders; they all pulled the ski-masks down over their faces. He took this as them being okay with the plan he had in mind, "Alright then, let's move."

Everyone jumped out of the van and slammed their doors shut, making hurried footsteps into Menace's yard. Bumpy was the first one up the steps and at the front door. He signaled for the goons to go around the back of the house, while he and Flocka took the front entrance. Once the goons were gone, Bumpy focused on the front door. He took a step back and launched his foot at the door's lock.

Boom!

Bumpy kicked open the front door. Right after, he and Flocka ran inside with their bangaz drawn, ready to wet up some shit. A second after, they heard the back door being kicked open. They didn't bother to look at the kitchen to see who was coming through the back door because they already knew it was their back up.

Bumpy and Flocka's heads snapped to the staircase hearing someone hurrying down them. They looked and met a nigga in a duster. It was Levon. As soon as he saw them masked up niggaz and they bangaz, he lifted his AK-47 and sprayed their asses. The slugs of his choppa chopped up the couch and surrounding furniture. Splitters, broken pieces of glass and stuffing from out of the couch was flying everywhere. Flocka and Bumpy dove in front of the couch just as the first wave of bullets cut through the living room, narrowly escaping the fury of the AK-47.

"Fuck is y'all niggaz, man?" Levon called out from the staircase.

"Who the fuck are you? And where the fuck is Menace?" Flocka called out from where he was hiding in front of the ruined couch.

"I came here looking for Menace and his bitch ass daddy, and I ran into you two bitches!" Levon responded, clutching his AK-47 with both hands as its barrel wafted with smoke. Seeing someone at the corner of his eye, he whipped his head around to see two masked up goons. These were the same niggaz that rushed the spot with Flocka and Bumpy. The first of the pair pointed his fat ass revolver at Levon and squeezed the trigger, the chamber of the fully loaded pistol twisted.

Blam! Blam!

The first bullet blew the middle of the wooden rail into splinters while the second one blew a big ass hole into the wall behind Levon. Levon's face contorted into a mask of hatred as he clenched his jaws and lifted his AK-47, taking aim. His choppa rattled to life once again and spat rapid fire, chopping the goons down. They danced super-fast on their feet as slugs chewed up their bodies, dotting the floor and furniture with their blood. A moment later, the goons fell out to the floor dead.

Flocka looked to his right and was surprised to see one of the dead goons a foot away from him. His eyes were big and vacant and his mouth was wide open, displaying most of his teeth.

"Yo', you know who this nigga is, man?" Bumpy asked Flocka, stealing his attention away from the dead goon lying beside him.

"Nah, I don't know this cocksucka, man, but he's on one." Flocka replied.

"He's got us by the balls, we don't stand a chance against this mothafucka with these puss' ass guns we got."

"I know, but if we go out, we go out blazin'."

"You mothafuckin' right. On the count of three, we come up from this couch givin' this ho ass nigga hell to pay. You got my back?" Bumpy looked into Flocka's eyes for assurance. Flocka's looked at him for a minute before responding. Although he agreed to go along with the plan that Bumpy had in mind, he was going to switch it up at the last minute. "Alright then," he said, holding up three fingers and dropping one with each number he called out. Once his last finger dropped, he scrambled to his feet and lifted his banga.

Seeing Bumpy about to pop Levon, Flocka pointed his banga at the back of his skull. He had it in mind to blow his brains out, so he could handle the money situation how he saw fit too. You see, it wasn't just about the loot, that nigga Flocka genuinely couldn't stand that mothafucka Bumpy. As Flocka aimed his gun at the little gangsta's dome piece, everything surrounding him went out of focus, besides his banga and Bumpy's head. He was just about to knock the gravy out of his biscuit, when the lights suddenly went out from Levon blasting on the power box.

As soon as the rapid fire ripped through the air, Bumpy ducked down and blindly fired his gun. He missed Levon with every shot as he hurried down the staircase, blazing shots back at his ass. The twin ran through the kitchen and out of the house, jumping down into the back yard's grass. He then ran across the lawn and hopped the back gate into the alley. He stuck his AK inside of his duster to conceal it and sped walked down the alley. Coming out of the alley, he spotted a 2008 Dodge Charger with a Hemi engine. Looking up and down the street for any oncoming vehicles or witnesses, he jogged across the street. When he reached the Charger, he busted its driver's window out with the butt of his AK. The alarm sounded off, so he opened the door quickly and disabled it. He then sat his AK on the front passenger's floor and hotwired the car. It came to life and he peeled off down the block.

****

Once Levon was gone, Flocka tried to grab Bumpy so they could get the fuck from out of Menace's house.

"Hold on. We can't get nowhere without the car keys, fool." Bumpy scrambled over to the goon that had dropped dead beside Flocka. Quickly, he went through the nigga'z pockets leaving loose dollars, wrinkled receipts and a couple of gold foil Magnum condoms behind. Once he found the key, he held it up in the light shining from outside so he could be sure that he had the right one. Realizing that he did, he hurriedly got to his feet and ran out of the house, with Flocka on his heels.

Police car sirens filled the air as Twelve headed to the area. Guns at their side, Bumpy and Flocka made hurried footsteps across the front lawn, looking all around them. The lights of some of the houses on the block started coming on, one by one. People were slowly emerging from out of their homes to see what was going on.

As soon as Bumpy and Flocka reached the sidewalk, two vehicles halted to stops in the middle of the residential block. They glanced over their shoulders to see, Menace, Shatira and Fonzell jumping out of their whips. They lifted their guns and started popping at Bumpy and Flocka as they fled towards their car.

"Bitch ass niggaz, gon' run up in me and my daddy's house? Y'all must think we pussy! Y'all got me fucked up!" Menace called out to the men as they ran for their lives, banging his tool off at them.

Blocka! Blocka! Blocka! Blocka!

His gun rang fierce and noisily, managing to knock off the side view mirror of a parked car. The gunfire also managed to blow holes into nearby parked vehicles as well. Angry, Menace lowered his gun and ejected his magazine. He let the magazine drop to the sidewalk and pulled one out of the back of his pocket, loading it up. While he was feeding the bottom of his tool, his crew was licking shots at who they didn't know were Bumpy and Flocka. Seeing that his crew could hold shit down, Menace ran into his house. Seeing that it was dark inside, he brandished his Bic lighter and flicked a flame. Using the light from the flame as a guide, Menace made his way upstairs and down the hallway. Once he entered his bedroom, he headed straight for the safe inside of his closet. He opened the safe and used the light to look at all of the money he'd stored away. Seeing that all of his loot was there and accounted for, Menace snatched a pillowcase from off a pillow that was lying on his bed. He then put his lighter into his pocket and walked over to the safe, he flapped the pillowcase open. Afterwards, he raked the money from out of the safe into the pillowcase. Once he'd cleared out the safe, he tied up the pillowcase and hoisted it over his shoulder. He closed the safe and then the closet's door.

Menace ran down the hallway and hurried down the staircase, hearing the gun battle outside along the way. When he finally made it outside, his crew was still banging it out with the masked up niggaz in the middle of the street. He saw one of the masked men hop into his van and swerve it around. As soon as he did, the shots from his crew shattered the windshield of the van and left gaping holes in the side of it as well. While this was happening, the masked man that hadn't gotten inside of the van yet, took cover behind a parked car and banged bang back at the opposition.

"Open the door, Blood! Open the door!" Flocka called out to Bumpy. He narrowed his eyelids as he tried to avoid the shattered glass of the parked car he had taken cover behind. The bullets from the opposition were tatting the vehicle and its broken glass was peppering his face. Still, he continued to lick shots at them fools on the other side of the street. He wasn't anybody's fool though, he knew that the level and intensity in which his foes were pumping out slugs that he'd eventually be murdered. He'd have to reload soon, so it was best to flee the gun battle before he found his ass bleeding to death in the middle of the street.

Keeping his head as low as he could, Bumpy flung open the door of the van. At this time, Menace was the only nigga left dumping at the van while the rest of his crew reloaded their guns. Seeing that it was best to escape his impending doom now, Flocka ran for the van as best as he could with a plastic leg, trading shots with Menace. As soon as his ass graced the front seat, he slammed the door shut and Bumpy sped away. At this time, Menace and everyone else had finished loaded their bangaz. The collective stood out in the middle of the residential block, licking shots at the back of the van. Their bullets pumped holes through the back of the fleeing vehicle and shattered its back windows. Once the van had gotten too far for them to keep shooting at, they lowered their smoking guns. Looking over their shoulders, they could see the flashing red and blue lights of Twelve in the distance heading in their direction. Acknowledging this, they jumped back into their respective cars and burned rubber away from the scene of the gun battle. Their speeding vehicles leaving broken glass and empty shell casings behind in the street.

****

"Yo', who the fuck were them niggaz back there?" Ducey asked as he doused the cars with gasoline from a red can. Menace, Shatira and Fonzell stood as lookouts as he handled the task at hand. They weren't worried about the automobiles having to be torched because they were stolen anyway. Besides, they couldn't keep those mothafuckaz if they wanted to. Both of the cars could be linked to the firefight so they had to go.

"I don't know, unc," Menace told him. "Delores and her punk ass sons are gone, so I don't have a clue as to what all that shit was about back there. Shit, when I went into the house I even saw two dead bodies lying on the floor."

"Really, son?" Fonzell asked with furrowed brows.

"Yep." Menace nodded as he placed his arm over Shatira's shoulders.

"Well, it isn't safe to be laid up there no more. At least not until I find out what the fuck is going on."

"I agree. That's why I'ma lay some cash on you to lamp up in a hotel 'til we finda new place to lay our heads. Matter of fact," he dug inside of the pillowcase and pulled out four stacks of blue faces, handing them to his father. Fonzell didn't waste any time storing the dead faces inside of his pockets.

"Thank you, son."

"Don't mention it, pop. We family, we gotta stick together."

"So, what's our next move?" Ducey asked as he splashed the flammable liquid onto the interior of one of the vehicles.

"You and me are gonna head back to the house." Fonzell answered. "I'm sure the block is crawling with One Time, and them boys are gonna want someone to answer for what happened."

"What're you going to tell them, pop?" Shatira inquired, with her head lying against Menace's chest and her arms wrapped around his waist.

"My usual line of bullshit." Fonzell replied.

"That's my old man." Menace cracked a smirk as he touched fists with Fonzell.

"Alright y'all, it's time to send these babies up in smoke." Ducey struck two matches across the black strip of a match book. They both hissed as they came away burning. He tossed one flaming match into each car. As soon as the matches touched the gas, a fire licked at the interior of the vehicles.

With the deed having been carried out, everyone exchanged daps and hugs, before going their respective ways.

****

"Fuuuuuck!" Big Meat screamed at the top of his lungs, his fists balled at his sides. Flocka and Bumpy was standing before him. They'd just given him the rundown of what had gone down at that nigga Menace's house.

Big Meat, with his head down and his hands behind his back, paced in front of his fireplace inside of the living room. He was dressed in black silk pajamas and a house robe. From the look on the big man's face, Flocka and Menace could tell that he had something on his mind.

"Question," Big Meat suddenly stopped and looked at Flocka.

"'Sup?" Flocka asked.

"Do you think Menace knows you were gunning for 'em?"

"Nah," Flocka shook his head as he replied. "He definitely doesn't know I was one of the fools bustin' at his ass. Hell, I'm sure he doesn't know old head was on his ass either." He referred to Bumpy who was standing beside him as he talked.

"Good, good, good," Big Meat said as he poured up a glass of cognac. Once he was done, he sat the square, clear bottle down on his desk top, then took a sip from his glass. "Here's what I want chu to do." he took the time to clear his throat with his fist to his mouth. "Tomorrow you're gonna holla at Menace and tell 'em you wanna meet somewhere. Tell 'em you wanna meet somewhere that there aren't many people, if there's any at all. Once he shows up, you crush his lil' punk ass. I just want the streets to know that Big Meat ain't the one to fuck with. Make an example out of the nigga, y'all got that?" He asked as he sat down behind his desk. He took another sip of alcohol as he waited for Flocka and Bumpy's response.

They both nodded. "Good. Y'all niggaz get ghost, I wanna be alone."

With that having been said, Flocka and Bumpy left their boss' mansion.

Chapter Four
The next day

Menace sat on the bed cleaning his gun, looking back and forth between his banga and Jumanji playing on the television's screen. While he was handling the task at hand, Shatira was taking a shower and singing Ella Mai's *Boo'd up.*

Feelings, so deep in my feelings
No, this ain't really like me
Can't control my anxiety
Feeling, like I'm touching the ceiling
When I'm with you I can't breathe
Boy, you do something to me

A smile spread across Menace's lips hearing his angel singing her heart out. It was something about her angelic voice that made his heart swell with love for her. He knew in his heart that she was the one for him and his choice to marry her was the greatest decision he'd ever made.

"Who you in there singing about, boo?" Menace called out to her.

"I'm singing about my baybee!" Shatira replied in a sing songy voice.

"You in love with me, baby?"

"Oh, I'm madly in love witchu, boy."

Still smiling, Menace went back to cleaning his gun while Shatira continued her singing. Hearing his cellular ringing and vibrating, he looked to the dresser and saw the name on the display. Seeing that it was Flocka, he sat his gun and brush down and answered it.

"What's good?" Menace said into his cell phone.

"Yo', what's up with it?" Flocka said as soon as his right-hand man came on the phone.

"My nigga, fuck you been? I been through wild shit out here. I needed my ace in my corner." He said with a hint of hostility in his voice.

"Nigga," he began shaking his head with his eyelids shut. "You don't know half the shit a nigga been through these last couple of days out here. You know that run me and Rondell made for Meat? Well, Rondell fucked around and got his shit split that night, and I lost my leg."

"Whaaaaaat? Get the fuck outta here." Menace said in disbelief.

"Yep." He nodded his head. "I seen you was blowin' up my jack, but I was so fucked up behind that shit I couldn't think straight."

"Fa sho', fa sho.'"

"Anyway, my nigga, what's been goin' on on yo' end?"

"Nothing much, really. You know me and lil' momma fucking with each other real tough."

"Real shit?"

"Yeah. We gon' get married and shit."

"Damn. Already?"

"Shiiiit. With the life we live, why waste time? Live fast die, die young. You know what I'm saying?"

"Sho' 'nough."

"You gon' be my best man when I jump the broom, right?"

"Bro, you ain't even gotta ask. You been my dawg since day one. I'ma be there when you get married."

Menace smiled hard hearing that. It felt good knowing his main man had his back. He'd never let him down and had always been there for him.

"That's what's up."

"Say, bruh, you think we can link up in the next half hour?"

"What's up, bro? What's going on?" Menace's forehead creased. He was genuinely concerned about his homeboy.

"I'll rap witchu once we meet up. You know where the Hawthorne Mall is, right?"

Menace finished his conversation with Flocka and disconnected the call.

A second later, Shatira came out of the bathroom with a towel wrapped around her. The upper half of her was still shiny from the water washing over her, although she'd dried off. She sat down on the bed and started lotioning herself up with the small bottle of lotion the hotel provided.

"Who was that, babe?" she asked she rubbed her legs down with lotion.

"Flocka. He wanna holla at me about something. We 'pose to link up at the Hawthorne mall."

"The Hawthorne mall?" her brows furrowed. "Isn't that place shut down?"

"Yeah. I figure he must be in trouble of something."

"Makes sense. Y'all are in the streets."

Menace continued to clean his gun. Once Shatira finished lotioning up, she slipped on her bra and panties. She then picked up her cellular and hit up Feebee. She studied her fingernails as the phone rang and rang, until it eventually went to voice mail. She left her girl a message and tossed the cell phone on the bed. Afterwards, she started putting on the clothes she was going to wear for the day.

"Did Flocka say anything about having spoken to Feebee, babe?" Shatira asked as she slipped her shirt over her head.

"Nah. He didn't mention ya girl. Why?" he askd, looking to see if he'd thoroughly cleaned his weapon. There was a little more dirt left inside of it so he continued to clean it.

"I been blowing her phone up, but she hasn't been answering my calls." She plopped down on the bed and started putting on her shoes.

"She's probably busy or some shit, baby. I'm sure she'll hit chu once she gets a minute."

"Yeah. You're probably right." Shatira told him. Still, her intuition told her that something was up with her best friend, but she chose to ignore it.

Girl, if you turn out to be okay, I'm going to kill your ass for having me worry.

****

Flocka posted up beside a big ass white van, smoking gas and taking in the scenery. He was supposed to be meeting Menace in the next couple of minutes. Sure, he could have gotten him to shoot his location to him but he knew him and his bitch was laying up at one of those expensive hotels, which more than likely had surveillance cameras, so he opted to holla at him someplace else. This other place was the very grounds he was standings on. The underground parking complex of the Hawthorne shopping plaza which had been closed down for quite some time.

Hearing the crunching of gravel coming from over his left shoulder, Flocka looked in that direction, to find Menace pulling up. A smile spread across his lips and he blew smoke out of the corner of his mouth. He watched as Menace stopped his car in front of him and hopped out, slamming the door closed behind him. The young nigga made his way around his car with a smile that matched his homeboy's. Menace slapped hands with Flocka and patted him on his back. Once he took a step back, Flocka dropped what was left of the blunt at his foot and mashed it out underneath his sneaker.

"That's wifey over there in the passenger seat?" Flocka inquired, looking at Shatira in the passenger seat. She flashed him a smile and waved at him. He threw his head back like, *What's up?* In response.

Menace glanced over his shoulder and turned back around to his right-hand man, saying, "Yeah, that's her. Once we say our vows shit gon' be official."

"That's what's up. My dawg gettin' on his grown man tip."

"I know, right? I'm waiting on my brotha to follow suit."

"Shiiiiiit, waitin' onna nigga like me you gon' be old and gray, bro. I can't settle down. I'd get bored wangin' the same broad over and over again. You know what I'm sayin'?"

"Yeah, youza mothafucking dog." he chuckled.

"Woof, woof, woof!" Flocka barked like a dog and grinned.

"You ain't shit, bro. But you still my nigga."

When he said that Flocka stopped grinning. It was like his conscience was eating away at him, for the scandalous shit he had in mind to do Menace. Flocka quickly shook that shit off his mental though. He had to do what he had to do if he was going to live to see another day.

"Sho' you right." he dapped him up.

"Limmie see yo' leg, man." Menace took a step back frowning, looking down at his homeboy's leg.

"Fa sho'." Flocka pulled up his jean leg and showed off his prosthetic, knocking on it. He then stood upright, grinning again.

"Bro, what the fuck happened?" Menace looked down at his leg in shock. He thought he was bullshitting when he told him he'd gotten his leg blown off, but he was wrong.

"It's a long story, my nigga. I'll tell you about it once you hop into the van." Flocka scowled and pulled out his gun swiftly, pointing it in Menace's face. Menace frowned up. His eyes darted back and forth between the banga in his best friend's hand and his eyes. He was trying to read him, to see if he was serious or not. "Stop playing, bro? Nah, you seriously." He looked deep into his eyes and knew his ass wasn't playing. "You fucking serious?"

"Dead ass. I'm sorry, bro." Flocka reached back and knocked on the van. The door of the van slid open. Bumpy was behind the wheel and a quartet of goons was in the back of the van. They were wearing ski-masks and toting AK-47s. Two of them hopped out, aiming their choppas at Menace. If he so much as sneezed they were going to light that ass up.

"Get in the van, nigga!" One of the goons grabbed Menace under his arm, pulling him toward the van.

"Get off me, Blood! Flocka, fuck is all this about?" Menace looked at his comrade for some understanding.

"You know what this shit is about, nigga? You sprayed the car, killed Rondell, left me a mothafuckin' cripple and took big homie's bags." Flocka lied, looking him straight in his eyes, face balled up in anger.

"What the fuck? I ain't rob Big Meat!"

"Ah, hell naw!" Shatira called out seeing what was going down. When everyone looked to her, she was pointing her gun out of the window and pulling the trigger.

Blowl!

The goon holding Menace's arm head snapped back, upon impact of the hollow tip bullet. His brain matter and blood sprayed out the back of his dome. He hit the ground wearing big eyes and a wide mouth. As soon as his dead body hit the surface, the rest of the goons pointed their AKs at Menace's car and opened fire. Shatira ducked down to the floor of the car, covering her head with her arms while still holding her gun. The car rocked back and forth as it was assaulted by heavy gunfire. The bullets from the AKs pelted it like hard rain. The vehicle's windows shattered and broken glass peppered Shatira.

While the AK-47s were making their ghetto music, Flocka was wrestling with Menace trying to get him inside of the van. If it wasn't for the fact that Menace had been his day-one, he would have shot him and tossed him inside of the van but he had mad love for him. You see, Flocka thought he had it in him to do Menace greasy, but apparently he was wrong.

"Pop that nigga and throw his ass in here, bruh!" Bumpy called out harshly from behind the wheel. "Don't kill 'em, but shoot 'em in his mothafucking leg or something! We gon' need his ass to tell us where that paypa at!"

With a grunt, Flocka cracked Menace upside the head with the butt of his gun, twice. The sharp blows didn't knock him out but they made him dizzy. Still, Menace fought to get away from Flocka. Seeing that Flocka was having trouble with his charge, Bumpy reached underneath the driver seat and produced a shiny chrome .357 Magnum revolver. He was about to mortally wound Menace so his goons could throw his ass into the van. Just as Bumpy was going to climb over the seats into the back of the van so he could get a good shot at Menace, he looked up and saw a light-skinned nigga in a duster, running up on them with an AK-47.

"Who the hell is that?" Bumpy asked no one in particular, forehead creasing.

At this time, the goons stopped firing on Menace's car which looked like Swiss cheese now. They ejected the empty banana clips from out of their choppas and loaded them with new ones. As they were lifting their AKs to spray the car again, Levon was jumping onto the trunk of the ruined vehicle. He smiled fiendishly and sprayed the goons, splashing their brain fragments and blood against the van. Once Levon had started shooting, Flocka tackled Menace to the ground. Doing so, he missed a wave of bullets that would have surely killed him.

"Ah, there yo' old punk-ass is." Levon turned his Ak-47 on Menace as he lay beneath Flocka. They both looked up at Levon with his choppa, realizing this was the end since he had the drop on them. "This is for my motha and my lil' brotha, bitch!"

Blowl! Blowl! Blowl!

Levon winced and lurched forward having taking slugs to his back. Swiftly, he swung around pointing his AK. He found Shatira at the end of his line of vision, pointing a gun up at him. When she saw herself staring down the barrel of Levon's AK-47, she dove to the ground.

Blatatatatatatat!

Shatira rolled out of the way of the bullets as they sprayed the ground where she once was, sending sprays of broken concrete into the air.

"Bitch, I'ma teach you to stay outta grown men bitness!" Levon winced, feeling the pain in his back from getting shot as he gripped his AK-47 with both hands. He was about to jump down to the ground and lay his murder game down on Shatira, when thunder rolled forward, loud and furiously.

Boc! Boc! Boc! Boc! Boc!

Flocka stood where he was and opened fired on Levon. Each shot propelled him backwards until he fell off the trunk of Menace's vehicle. Having heard his body smack down on the ground out of sight, Flocka lowered his gun and looked to Menace. He found him mad dogging him and pointing a gun at his chest, ready to heat his ass up.

Flocka and Menace mad dogged one another. Menace wondering if he could shoot Flocka or not, and Flocka wondering if he was going to shoot or not.

"What are you doing, baby? Shoot 'em! Fucking shoot 'em!" Shatira called out to Menace as he slowly rose to his feet, still holding her gun.

At that moment, Bumpy sped off leaving the door of the van open.

Flocka and Menace continued to stare one another down. *Fuck,* Menace thought to himself as he shut his eyelids and lowered his gun. Like, Flocka, he couldn't find it in himself to pop his best friend. As soon as Flocka realized Menace wasn't going pop him, he took off running to catch up with the van. Reaching the van, he tucked his gun at the small of his back and dove inside of it.

"Unh!" Flocka landed hard on the floor of the van. He then turned over, staring out of the open door. He saw Shatira helping Menace to his feet. Once Menace was standing tall, he looked in Flocka's direction for a minute. The two best friends held one another's gaze for a while. That is, until Flocka got up and pulled the van's door shut.

****

"Why didn't you pop 'em, bae?" Shatira asked Menace after helping him to his feet. She couldn't believe he didn't smoke Flocka's ass when he had the drop on him.

Menace was holding Flocka's gaze at the time Shatira questioned him. It wasn't until Flocka slammed the door of the van shut and cut off their eye contact, that he focused all of his attention on her. "I couldn't. I couldn't bring myself to do it, slim. Me and bro gotta long history. He's as good as blood in my eyes. Oh, shit!" Menace brushed her aside and made his way over to the side of his swiss cheesed car, gun outstretched. He moved around the vehicle cautiously, with Shatira at his rear. She'd picked up on what had grabbed his attention. Levon! When Flocka blasted on his ass he fell off the trunk of the car, but they never checked to see if he was still there.

When Menace and Shatira made it to the other side of the car, Levon had disappeared. In fact, the only thing in the space where he'd fallen were dots of blood and his AK-47. Seeing the blood, Menace and Shatira exchanged glances of shock. They then lowered their bangaz at their side.

"Mothafucka just upped and vanished in the air, like magic." Menace declared.

"Shit crazy. I didn't even see 'em leave." Shatira claimed.

Hearing the sounds of police sirens, Menace and Shatira snapped their necks over their shoulder. At the end of their line of vision, they saw several police cars racing across their paths, heading to their location no doubt.

"Come on. We gotta get up from outta here!" Menace grabbed her hand and ran toward his bullet riddled vehicle. They jumped inside of his ride and pulled off, leaving dust in their wake.

That night

Levon pulled the Charger inside the parking lot of Dynasty Inn motel and killed its engine. He hopped out from behind the wheel and slammed the door shut behind him. He then made his way to the trunk of the car and lifted it. Holding the trunk open with one outstretched hand, he grabbed the bag of goods he'd purchased from the AM/PM gas station from up the street. Wincing, he slammed the door shut and made his way inside of the motel's lobby. He pushed the glass door opened and left a bloody hand impression on it. The glass door shut behind him and the clerk frowned up, seeing he'd stained the glass. Levon glanced at him with a *So, fucking what* expression across his face and kept on to his destination. The clerk adjusted his glasses as he frowned up at him. His eyes followed Levon until he was out of his sight. He then balled up some newspaper and grabbed a bottle of Windex, walking out from behind the counter. He opened the side door and came from out of the bulletproof casing of the check-in station. Stopping before the bloody hand impression on the glass door, he sprayed it with the Windex and went on to wipe it. The blood smeared at first, but the more he wiped the more of the stain disappeared.

The motel Levon was holing up at was one of the more shittier ones in Gardena. It was a seedy establishment that housed everyone from pimps to dope fiends. They didn't give a fuck who you were or what you did in the privacy of your room, just as long as you paid for your stay and didn't damage the furnishings they provided. This was the reason why Levon had picked the spot to stay in while he launched his attack on Menace and Shatira. He knew the owner of the motel wouldn't put his nose in his business, so the shady location was the perfect domicile for him.

As soon as Levon entered his room he flipped on the light switch, sat his bag on the dresser and removed his duster. He threw his duster across the bed and unstrapped his bulletproof vest, wincing as he took it off. He held the body armor up to the lighting inside of the room and rays shined through the bullet holes in the back of it. Staring up at the holes, Levon couldn't help thinking how lucky he was to still be alive. This had been the second attempt on his life since that bullet had skinned the side of his head back in the woods.

Levon sat the bulletproof vest down on the bed alongside his duster. He then pulled off his T-shirt, tossed it aside and grabbed the bag he'd sat on the dresser. He made his way inside of the bathroom, where he'd left the light on before he'd left. He sat his bag on the toilet lid and examined his injuries in the bathroom's mirror, wincing as he touched the areas. Covering his back were purplish red bruises from where Shatira had shot him. When he turned to face the mirror, he saw a bloody gaping hole in his upper chest area, off to the side. Seeing the butt of something copper inside his wound, he leaned forward for a closer look. That's when he discovered that what he was staring at was the bullet fragment he'd been shot with.

"There you are, you lil' fucka. So, it's you that's been giving me all that hell, huh? Well, I'm gonna have to get chu out." Levon snatched a towel from off the rack, folded it up to his liking, and bit down hard on it. He then took the time to turn on the faucet of the bathroom sink and rinsed his hands, watching the blood turn pink as it swirled down the drain. Afterwards, he cleaned around his wound with a washcloth. Next, he removed the items he'd need from out of the bag. A bottle of 100 proof Vodka, gauze and tape.

Levon twisted the cap off the liquor bottle and poured some on his gaping wound. As soon as the alcohol mingled with his opened flesh, he squeezed his eyelids shut and bit down hard on the towel. Veins bulged in his forehead and up his neck, looking like they were about to burst from his muffled screams. Quickly, he took the towel out of his mouth and took the Vodka bottle to the head, guzzling it. His throat moved up and down as he partook in the alcohol beverage, spilling some of it down his chin. He took the bottle from his mouth and wiped his lips with the back of his hand, hissing from the fiery liquor coating his throat.

"Whoooo!" Levon sat the bottle down on the toilet lid. He dried the area around his wound with the towel he'd bitten down on. Having tossed the towel aside, he placed the gauze over his wound and taped it down. Once he'd finished, he grabbed his bag and picked up the bottle of Vodka. He turned the clear bottle up, drinking from it as he headed back into his room.

Levon sat down on the bed and sat the bottle of Vodka down on the small desk. He then pulled out his cellular phone and hit up his homeboy. He placed the cell phone to his ear and as it rung, he dumped out the contents of the bag on the bed. Wrinkled bills of all denominations, some of which were stained with blood, spilled out onto the bed. Levon tossed the bag aside and began sorting through the money, matching bills up. The money he'd dumped out onto the bed was the loot he'd stuck up a store for when he got the items he needed to take care of his wound.

"Wango, what's up with it? Ain't shit, chillin'." Levon chuckled at something his acquaintance said as he continued to sort through the bills on his bed. "Aye, listen, I needa get my hands onna yoppa, asap. Yeah, I got some busta ass niggaz I needa straighten out."

****

Fonzell outstretched his arm across the kitchen table. Ducey placed the syringe of dope between his teeth and stood up from his chair, unbuckling his belt. He pulled the belt free from his loops and pulled his chair closer to Fonzell. He then sat back down, looping the belt around Fonzell's arm and buckling it. He then held his arm, turning it from left to right searching for a vein. He leaned in for a closer look once he thought he found one, smacking it trying to make it pronounced. Fonzell looked down at his vein as Ducey tried to make it form. He balled his fist tighter than he had before the belt was buckled around it and the vein stood out amongst his scab riddled arm.

"There she go, stubborn lil' black bitch ain't she?" Ducey said of the vein, clenching the syringe between his teeth, which partially altering his words. He held

Fonzell's arm with one hand and used the other to take the syringe from out of his mouth. Focusing his attention on the thick vein at the center of his partner's arm, Ducey brought the needle toward it. The tip of the needle was about to penetrate the vein, when Fonzell's cellular rung.

Fonzell was going to ignore the call because he wanted to get faded, but something told him he should see who was hitting him up. With that thought in mind, he held up a finger for Ducey to give him a minute. Ducey leaned back in his chair, watching him pull his cell phone from out of his pocket. He looked at the display of the cellular frowning up. He didn't know who the fuck the number calling him belonged to.

"Who is it?" Ducey asked, bouncing his leg up and down impatiently, as he scratched his chest. He was hoping Fonzell would hurry up with his phone call becaue he was trying to get high ASAP.

"I don't know." Fonzell replied, eyes still focused on the screen of the cell phone. He was trying to decide if he should answer the call or not.

"Well, if you don't know who it is, fuck 'em! I been trying get nice all mothafucking day."

"Nah, this could be my boy. I gotta take this one, gon' and do you, Ducey."

"Hey, no argument there." Ducey unbuckled the belt and removed it from Fonzell's arm. He put the belt around his arm and buckled it, searching for a vein in his arm so he could shoot up.

Fonzell answered the call.

"What's up?" Fonzell spoke into his cell phone.

"Your punk ass son." A familiar voice responded.

A surprised expression crossed Fonzell's face. He hadn't heard the voice on the jack in almost twenty years.

The surprised look on his face disappeared, being replaced by an angry one.

"Watch how you speak about my boy now."

"Just what in the fuck are you gonna do if I don't, huh? Notta goddamn thang, ya dope fiend. I suggest you recall who had the respect out in these streets."

Big Meat's slick tongue had Fonzell as hot as an oven. He gripped his cell phone so tight that he heard the plastic crack on it.

"Fuck you want, man?" Fonzell asked, heatedly. He glanced over his shoulder to see if Ducey was listening; he wasn't. Ducey's ass was leaned back in the chair, letting the dope take him to a beautiful place.

"Your boy stole three-hundred and something dollars from me. And if I don't get it back, I'ma do to him, what I did to you so many years ago. The same goes for that lil' punk ass ho he's running with, too."

"What? My son ain't gotta steal nothing from yo' ass. Jr. makes his own dough."

"Which is why I don't understand why he'd wanna rip me off." Big Meat said. "You'd think that seeing you every day would remind 'em of the consequences of fucking with what belongs to me, but I guess it hasn't."

"Are you threatening my son's life?"

" I'm threatening all of your lives, nigga! 'Cause I know yo' strung out ass more than likely convinced 'em to lift them dollars."

"Look, here, bruh," Fonzell began. "I didn't convince my son to take a goddamn thang from you, and he didn't take shit from you either. You can either choose to believe it, or let it pass like a fart in the wind. Either way, it doesn't make any difference to me, but you fucked up coming for my boy. I love that one there dearly...more than myself."

"Nigga, what's that 'pose to mean to me? You love dope more than you love yourself, you pathetic piece of shit!"

"Why don't we take this shit to the streets, so you can see just how much of a pathetic piece of shit I really am?"

"Hahahahahahahahahahaha!" Big Meat laughed hard as hell. "My nigga, Fonzell, where is all of this heart coming from? Niggaz in our circle know you for playing the guitar and singing love songs. Since when did you start busting yo' gun in these streets?"

"Since I been in 'em, bitch boy. I'ma come see 'bout cha, ya hear?" Fonzell disconnected the call and tossed his cell phone upon the couch. He then rose up and walked to the bathroom. He turned on the faucet water, allowing the cool water to spill inside of the sink. He cupped his hand underneath the water and splashed it on his face, twice.

Fonzell dried his face off on one of the towels on the rack. He then walked out of the bathroom and back inside of the kitchen. He found Ducey still feeling the full effects of the dope, but he didn't pay that nigga any mind. Nah, he had some thinking he needed to do, so that's what he did. He paced the floor, thinking and massaging his chin. Once he figured out what he was going to do with his current situation, he snapped his fingers and grabbed his jacket. It took some time for him to get it on being that he only had one hand, but he managed.

"Yo', Ducey, I'm finna busta move, fam, but I'll be right back." Fonzell pulled a beanie over his head and adjusted it as he walked toward the door. He pulled the door open and glanced over his shoulder at Ducey. He was still laid back in the chair, high as a mothafucka.

Fonzell closed the door on his way out. As of now, he was headed out to grab a very important item that would aid him in the night's mission.

****

Fonzell stood below the freeway on a slick, grimy surface, at the center of a quartet of barrels of burning shards of wood. The flames licked at the shards of wood sticking out of the barrels causing them to glow a golden orange. Embers floated from off of the shards and swarmed in the air like bumble bees on a warm summer day.

Having just finished lighting all of the shards of wood occupying the barrels, Fonzell tossed the lighter fluid aside and slipped the Bic lighter he'd used inside of his pocket. Right after, his cellular was ringing and he was pulling it out to answer it. He pressed the button to receive the call and placed the cell phone to his ear.

"What's up, Ducey? Yeah, I see 'em now." Fonzell spoke through the earbud in his ear. Looking up from where he was standing, he saw a Lincoln Town car driving in his direction. "Okay. Good. I appreciate chu handling this for me, homeboy. I owe you one. Cool. Peace." he disconnected the call and tossed the device aside. He watched as the Lincoln Town car stopped, and Bumpy hopped out of the driver's seat. The little gangsta slammed the door shut and walked around to the opposite side of the vehicle, pulling the back door open. He then stepped aside and allowed Big Meat to step out, one foot at a time. "It's show time!"

Fonzell pulled off his beanie and slung it aside. He removed his jacket, letting it fall to the ground. Next, he pulled off his T-shirt and left his hairy chest exposed. Once he dropped his shirt to the surface, he focused his attention back on Big Meat and Bumpy. He observed Bumpy duct taping Big Meat's left arm against his body. When he saw him doing this, he frowned up wondered what the two men were up to. Once Bumpy was finished taping his boss' arm against his body, he stepped aside and allowed the hulking man a clear path to his rival.

As Big Meat made his way toward Fonzell, the dope fiend noticed what he was wearing. The big mothafucka was dressed in a black wife beater, gray camouflage pants and boots. Before he knew it, Big Meat was standing in front of him.

"I take it you wondering why I got my arm taped to me, huh?" Big Meat asked Fonzell, but he didn't respond to him. So he went on to tell him why he had Bumpy tape his arm to him. "Well, the way I see it, you only got one arm. So, this would be a handicap match. I had my right-hand there," he nodded to Bumpy, who was posted up by the car. The little gangsta had his arms folded across his chest, and his eyes were focused on his boss and Fonzell. "Tape my arm to me so we'd have an even playing field."

Fonzell nodded, liking the fact that Big Meat was giving him a fair one. He could have come out there with both hands and probably beat him to a bloody pulp, but whipping his ass straight up was more honorable. "I can respect that."

"I thought that chu would."

"Tell me this though," Fonzell began. "How do I know that if I'm the victor in this squabble that the tiny gangsta over there isn't going to pop me?"

Big Meat looked over his shoulder at Bumpy, and then turned back around to Fonzell, answering him, "I gave him orders to fallback. It's just me and you out here, homie. And only one of us is leaving from underneath this freeway alive."

"You got that shit right." Fonzell's eyebrows arched.

With that having been said, Big Meat and Fonzell got into their respective fighting stances. They moved in on each other, trying to decide when was the right time to strike. Fonzell was the first to act, throwing jabs at Big Meat. The big man ducked and maneuvered around the attack. When Fonzell drew his fist back, Big Meat saw him about to kick him in the side. He caught him by his ankle, leaving Fonzell bouncing up and down on his last leg. The big man smiled wickedly, and Fonzell whipped around swiftly. The slender man slammed the heel of his sneaker into his foe's jaw, sending a mist of blood spraying out of his mouth. Big Meat stumbled aside hurriedly, bumping into one of the barrels of wood shards and spilling its contents. He hollered aloud feeling the sweltering hot barrel against his flesh. He gritted his teeth to combat the pain as he got back upon his feet, finding a pouncing Fonzell ready for more.

"You got that." Big Meat wiped the dripping blood from his bottom lip, with the back of his fist. He then rejoined the fight, moving in on Fonzell, throwing punches at him. Fonzell deflected the punches with his stump, but he left himself vulnerable to another attack. Seeing an opening, Big Meat kicked him in the side of his kneecap, dropping him down to one leg. He then punched him dead in his grill, bloodying his mouth. He followed up, punching him in the jaw, and then back handing him. He kicked him in the stomach and once he doubled over, a sharp kick in the chin lifted him off his feet. Fonzell landed hard on his back, lying there staring up at the bottom of the freeway underpass. He was a little dizzy, his cheek was bruised black and blue, and his teeth were bloody.

"Come on now, get up! Get cho old dope fiend ass up!" Big Meat urged him, motioning for him to stand up on his feet. "This what chu called me up for, right? You wanted to shoot the fair one? Well, get that ass up, and come get some!"

Fonzell lifted his head up from the ground and shook off his dizzy spell. Slowly, he got upon his feet. Once he was standing upright, with his fist before his eyes, Big Meat smiled evilly.

"Yeah, that's what I'm talking about. Come on with it!" Big Meat told him.

Fonzell moved in with determination to beat Big Meat's ass written across his face. He then threw a combination of punches and tried to kick him, but his attacks failed miserably. Frustrated, Fonzell started swinging wildly on Big Meat, but he wasn't able to connect. The big man punched him in his rib cage, cracked him in his jaw, backhand slapped him, and then kicked him in the chest. The force from the impact sent Fonzell stumbling backwards, bumping into one of the barrels. He knocked over the barrel and spilled its contents. Burning shards, trash and embers went flying everywhere.

"Uhhhh!" Fonzell hit the ground hard, bumping the side of his head. He winced and lay there for a second. Then, a moment later, he was scrambling to his feet. Once he'd gotten to his feet, he threw his head up. Fonzell was surprised to see Big Meat charging at him, holding one of the glowing wood shards with a rag. The big man whacked Fonzell across the head, on the opposite side of his face, and then swung the wood shard down against the top of his head. Upon impact, burning splinters and embers went flying everywhere. Fonzell collapsed to the ground. Big Meat looked down at him as he breathed heavily. Noticing that Fonzell was barely conscious and moaning in pain, Big Meat threw what was left of the splinter aside. He then ripped the duct tape that bound his arm to his body off, with three strong tugs. The big man casted the duct tape he'd ripped off to the side.

"Nigga fucked my bitch, hadda baby by her...I still owe you for that!" Madness danced in Big Meat's eyes as he licked his lips. He got down on his knees and wrapped his muscular arms around Fonzell's leg, gritting his teeth as he applied pressure to it. His arms shook slightly as he applied more and more pressure to Fonzell's leg.

Snappp

"Raaahhhhhh!" Fonzell's eyelids peeled wide open as he screamed at the top of his lungs. When Big Meat left his leg it was twisted at a funny angle. The big man grabbed his other leg. Again, he applied pressure to his leg, and it broke. *Craaaack!* "Aaaaaaahhhhhhh!"

"Tonight, you learn the meaning of pain." Big Meat wrapped his legs and arms around Fonzell's right arm. The big man gritted his teeth as he applied pressure to Fonzell's limb. There was an eerie crackling sound, before the man's arm broke in half. *Snappp!*

"Aaaaaaaaah!" Fonzell screamed even louder than he did the last time.

Big Meat broke Fonzell's other arm and let it drop limply to the ground. As he screamed out in agony, the big man sat down on his back and wrapped his arms around his neck. After making sure his biceps had locked Fonzell's neck in place, Big Meat snapped his victim's neck violently. Instantly, Fonzell's pained cries were silenced...forever. The big man released his enemey's neck and rose to his feet. He looked down at him with hatred in his eyes. He snarled and spit on him. Right after, he stomped his head into the ground for good measure.

Big Meat looked up from his handiwork and motioned Bumpy over to him. Once he was standing before him, he told him what to do. "Look, I want chu to take this mothafucka'z body to the crematory over in Inglewood that White Mike runs. Have that nigga burn the body to ashes. I'll hit 'em up and let 'em know you're coming."

"Gotcha." Bumpy nodded. "You rolling out with me or what?"

"Nah, I'ma make my way up to ground and catch an Uber home."

"Alright, then." he dapped up his boss.

Big Meat walked from out of the underpass and headed toward ground, which was street level. As he was walking away, Bumpy was busying himself with Fonzell's dead body. He drug the dead nigga'z corpse over to the Lincoln Town car and dumped his body into its trunk. After he slammed the trunk shut, he jogged over to the driver's door and opened it. Jumping inside behind the wheel, he fired up the engine and pulled off.

Tranay Adams

Chapter Five

Bumpy pushed the Lincoln Town Car, gangsta leaning and blowing smoke at the windshield. He nodded his head to some Curtis Mayfield, taking in the scenery as he drove through the Los Angeles streets. The mothafucka was so laid back, you wouldn't have thought he had a dead body in the trunk of his fucking car, but he did. What he was doing wasn't anything out of the ordinary for him, especially since he'd started working for Big Meat. Hell, this was like any other day at the office for him. Homeboy had gotten rid of more bodies than he could count on both hands, so his current situation wasn't a big deal for him.

Bumpy glanced up in the rear view mirror as he was blowing gas. His hooded eyelids snapped wide open when he saw a police car behind him, flashing its colorful lights. Quickly, he smashed out what was left of the blunt he was smoking, and swallowed it. He made an ugly ass face having tasted the disgusting ashes and leaf of the blunt. Popping open the glove-box, he grabbed the knock off Calvin Klein cologne stored inside. He sprayed around inside of the Town Car, and then he sprayed himself. Once he was done, he tossed the cologne back inside of the glove-box and smacked it closed. Afterwards, he looked himself over in the rearview mirror. His eyes looked sleepy and red webbed. The nigga still looked high as shit.

"Fuck man!" Bumpy punched the ceiling, mad at himself for getting high on the job. He looked through the inventory inside of the glove-box again and discovered a Visine bottle. He smiled once he had it in his hand, but when he took a closer look at it. He saw that there was only a drop. Balancing the steering wheel as best as he could, Bumpy held his head back a little and dripped some of the clear liquid from the small Visine bottle into his eye. Bringing his head back down, he blinked his eyelids rapidly and stuffed the small empty bottle between the driver seat and console.

Bumpy continued to blink his eyelids like he had something in his eye. Once he stopped blinking, he looked himself over to make sure he didn't have any incrimination evidence on him. Seeing that he was straight, he turned the music down and pulled over on the right shoulder of the street. Once he'd turned the car off, he cleared his throat with his fist to his mouth and started practicing the upbeat, proper accent he wanted to engage the officer with.

Bumpy looked into the side view mirror and watched the tall Asian cop unboard his police car and slam the door closed behind him. The cop adjusted his glasses as he made his way towards the Lincoln Town Car. Once he reached the driver's window, he motioned for Bumpy to let the window down. Bumpy obliged him and presented him with his greatest smile.

"How are you doing tonight, officer?" Bumpy asked him, jovially.

The officer didn't say anything; he was too busy studying the interior of the vehicle behind his glasses. Seeing him do this really pissed Bumpy off. He really wanted to cuss his ass out, but he was sure it would land him in hot water, and the mothafucka would be going through his car. The last thing he wanted was this cocksucka to find Fonzell's dead ass in his trunk.

The officer sniffed the air. Instantly, his forehead wrinkled and he looked to Bumpy.

"I smell weed."

"Weed? Really? That's odd, 'cause I don't smoke." Bumpy said, looking like he was really surprised the officer smelled weed lingering inside of his car.

"Hmmph." the officer griped, not believing him. "License and registration, please."

"Alright." Bumpy leaned over to the glove-box, causing his shirt to rise and reveal the gun on his hip. Instantly, the police officer snatched his handgun from out of his holster. He pointed it at Bumpy as he gripped it with two hands.

"Freeze!"

Bumpy stiffened up. His eyes stretched open and his brows furrowed. He wondered what the fuck was going on. *Shit,* he mouthed to himself as he remembered he was packing. The mothafucka was so high he'd forgotten he had his banga on him.

****

A worried Big Meat sat inside of his study sipping cognac and staring at his throwaway cellular. It had been hours since Bumpy had went to discard Fonzell's body, and he still hadn't heard from him. He spent the past hour blowing up his cell phone, but he'd yet to return any of his calls. In his heart of hearts he knew something had gone wrong, but he was still hoping for the best.

Big Meat sat his cell phone down on his desk top after looking at it for what he thought was the millionth time. He lay back in his executive chair and took another casual sip of his expensive liquor. As soon as he took a breath and his shoulders slumped, his cell phone rang. Swiftly, Big Meat sat up in his chair and sat his glass of cognac down on the desk top. He picked up his cellular and took a look at the display. The number wasn't listed, but he went ahead and answered the call anyway.

"Yeah?" Big Meat said into the device.

"Yo', I got locked up on some bullshit. I'ma need you to get me an attorney. ASAP." Bumpy replied.

"Say no more."

"Peace."

Big Meat disconnected the call and set the cell phone down on the desk top. In a fit of rage, he threw the glass of alcohol at the wall. The glass exploded upon impact, sending broken glass and cognac everywhere.

****

Menace was devastated when he'd gotten a call that night to identify a body that was believed to be his father. On his way over to view the body he prayed to God that it wouldn't be his old man. For as long as his old man had ran the streets robbing, stealing and beating folks over the head to pay for his habit, he'd never gotten so much as a hair harmed on his head. In other words, he'd never suffered any consequences for the game he chose to play. But some how Menace felt like this time would be different for his old man. Something told him that the chickens had came home to roost, and his father had gotten his just due.

The morgue was exceptionsally cold when Menace and Shatira entered. The medical examiner led them over to a table at the far corner of the room. He gave them a look to see if they were ready for what they were about to see. Menace looked him square in the eyes and nodded. The examiner returned the gesture and took a deep breath. He then pulled the sheet back from the body, exposing Fonzell's face and upper body. His neck and arms were swollen from having been broken. His eyelids were shut and his lips were rigid. He looked like he was asleep, but his food stamp blue complexion betrayed the fact that he was dead.

"This your old man, kid?" the medical examiner asked Menace.

"Yeah, that's him." Menace said as he stared down at his father, eyes filling with tears. Seeing the hurt in his eyes, Shatira stood beside him and rubbed his back soothingly. She then leaned her head against his shoulder.

"I'll give you a minute." The medical examiner said before making his departure.

"Goddamn, pop. Goddamn." Menace said in a hushed tone as he stroked his father's forehead. He shut his eyelids and tears jetted down his cheeks. Sniffling, he leaned down and kissed his old man on his forehead. He then placed his cheek against his cheek and threw his arm around his neck. He sobbed long, loud and hard as he held him, dripping his teardrops on the metal slab his father was stretched out upon.

"It's going to be okay, bae...everything is gonna be all right." Shatira assured him as tears trickled from her eyes. She wiped them away with her curled finger and sniffled. Seeing her man in so much emotional pain brought a great sadness to her. Not only that, Fonzell's dead body made her think of her own deceased father. She knew exactly how Menace felt and she was going to do everything she could to help him through his father's tragic death.

"I love you, pop. I love you so much." Menace said as he took his cheek away from his father's, dripping teardrops over his old man's face. He wiped his eyes on his sleeve and then kissed Fonzell on the cheek. He draped the sheet back over his father's body and turned around to Shatira, holding her tight. In that moment, he didn't give a fuck about keeping up his hardcore gangsta image. He just wanted to be held while he bawled his eyes out.

"I got chu, bae. I got chu, now and forever." Shatira swore as she held him in her arms, sweeping her hand up and down his back, affectionately.

The next day

"So, what's it looking like for my boy?" Big Meat asked Mr. Goldsmith, Bumpy's attorney, as he sat back in his executive chair and crossed his legs, nestling his hands in his lap.

Goldsmith unbottoned his suit and sat down in the chair before the desk. He then whipped out his handkerchief and patted the beads of sweat from his forehead. He was a tall chubby man with bulldog cheeks and a receding hairline and a balding spot at the back of his head. The Jewish attorney had been providing Big Meat with his services since he graduated from ounces to bricks. The two of them had a lovely business relationship, and looked at one another as friends.

"It's not looking good. It's not looking good at all for Mr. Holden." Goldsmith told him, straight up. "They caught him with a dead body in the trunk and an unregistered firearm. This is will be his third strike, so he's looking at never getting out again should he be convicted."

"Shiiiiit." Big Meat looked away as he massaged his chin, thinking on the situation. He then looked back up at Goldsmith. "Is there anything you can do for 'em?"

"Unfortunately, my hands are tied here." he answered. "Listen, I'm not trying to plant any seeds in your head, but I think I oughta ask. How well do you know Mr. Holden? And are you sure you can trust him? I mean, can you trust that he'll keep his mouth shut and do his time, if sentenced?"

"I know Bumpy just as well as I know myself." Big Meat said. "As long as I have known 'em he's been a stand up nigga. There isn't any flaws in his character, as far as I can see. Why?"

"Oh, nothing. Nothing at all."

"Spit it out." He insisted.

"Well," Goldsmith began. "The way I see it, why take a chance with this guy? He knows too much about you."

Big Meat angled his head and stared at Goldsmith for a minute, frown fixed on his face. The air around them was so quiet you could hear a pin drop. He licked his lips and sat up in his chair.

"Mr. Goldsmith, are you suggesting I have my best friend killed? A man I've known since before I could piss straight?"

"Not at all. In fact, forget everything that I just told you." he removed his glasses and fogged the lenses, cleaning them with his handkerchief. "All I want you to know, is I am going to continue to provide the best legal counsel to Mr. Holden." he slipped the glasses back on and adjusted them to his liking. "I assure you I am going to fight for him like he was you behind those walls." Having said that, Mr. Goldsmith stood up and buttoned his suit, outstretching his hand. "Good afternoon, Mr. Stevens."

Big Meat looked at Goldsmith's hand for a moment. He then leaned forward and shook his hand. The big man lay back in his chair, watching his attorney's back as he headed for the door. As soon as he pulled the door open, he called him back.

"Mr. Stevens?" Goldsmith looked upon him like *What's up?*

"Do you know anyone that can assure that I *stay* a free man?"

Goldsmith cracked a grin and shut the door. He then made his way back over to Big Meat to discuss the situation at hand.

Later that day

Yung sat behind the wheel of his Nissan, watching people coming and going from Ralph's supermarket. While observing the patrons he removed his glasses and fogged its lenses with his hot breath. He then whipped out a handkerchief and wiped the lenses clean of his fingerprints and smudges. Once he'd finished, he slid the glasses back on and adjusted them to his liking. After a while, he slumped in his seat having grown tired of waiting for whomever he was looking for. It wasn't until he saw a tall, white dude with a muscular physique pushing his shopping cart out of the store that he sat up. His neck slowly craned as he moved his head, following him as he crossed the parking lot.

Yung reached into the backseat and grabbed a golf club. He opened the driver's door and jumped out, slamming the door shut behind him. His eyes were zeroed in on the muscle bound meat-head pushing the shopping cart. Old boy was whistling Dixie like he didn't have a care in the world, looking around for his vehicle. Once he found it, he pulled out his car keys and unlocked it, with a push of a button on the small remote control. The locks unlocked on a blue 2014 Chevrolet Suburban. "Aye, you,

you buff neck faggot!" Yung pointed at the buff man with his golf club. The dude's eyebrows rose and he pointed to his chest with his thumb like, *You talking to me?* "Yeah, you, you piece of shit! You fucked my wife up the ass, didn't ya?"

"What? What are you talking about? Dude, I'm gay." the muscular man reasoned. He held up his hands and slowly stepped away from Yung when he saw the golf club in his hand.

"Bullshit! You can deny it all you want, but I seen it with my own goddamn eyes!" Yung spat flames. He was playing the role of a pissed off husband beautifully. The mothafucka deserved an Oscar. "Now, I'm getting divorced! I'll have to split half my assets, and I'll probably only see my daughter on the fucking weekends'cause of you! Thanks a fucking lot, pal!"

Yung ran up the hood of the Tahoe and jumped on top of the roof of it. He then took his golf club into both of his hands and parted his legs for balance.

"Hey, what the fuck are you doing?" the muscular man called up to Yung.

"You fucked up my shit! Now I'm gonna fuck up yours!" Yung swore, cocking the golf club back over his head. He then swung it downward with all of his might. The golf club made a sickening crunch sound as it slammed into the windshield of the Tahoe, cracking the glass into a cobweb. Yung cocked the golf club back over his head and swung it down again, cracking the windshield some more.

"Oh, my God! What the fuck is your problem, man? Have you gon' mad?" the muscular man clutched either side of his head, looking up at Yung attack his truck. He couldn't believe the thinly built, five-foot-seven Chinese man was destroying his vehicle.

By this time, people that were coming and going to Ralph's super market had stopped in their tracks. They were all staring up at Yung as he whacked the big body truck with the golf club. Shock was written across their faces. Their eyes were bugged and their mouths were hanging open.

"Mad? Who's mad, I'm fucking insane!" Yung screamed at the top of his lungs, spit flying from off his lips. He turned red in the face and the vein at this temple threatened to burst. He swung his golf club at the Tahoe's windshield over and over again, continuing his assault. Small particles of glass peppered his face and clothing, as he vandalized the SUV.

Stopping for a second, Yung breathed huskily and wiped the sweat from his forehead. He heard the police car sirens heading his way, but he didn't give a mad ass fuck. He had a job to do, and nothing or no one was going to stop him from doing it.

Yung jumped down onto the hood of the Tahoe and then to the asphalt. He started beating on the hood with the golf club, knocking big ass dents in it and shit. He then busted the headlights. The bystanders didn't do shit but watch him decimate the vehicle, and whisper about the proceedings amongst one another. Some of them mothafuckaz took out their cell phones and started filming the shit so they could load it up on social media.

"Jesus-fucking-Christ, look at what you're doing to my baby! Stop, stop, you crazy son of a bitch!" the muscular man shouted. He damn near turned burgundy in the face from shouting. The veins covering his forehead and body bulged.

Yung stopped beating on the truck and turned around to the vehicle's owner, pointing the golf club at him, shouting back, "Fuck. Youuuuuu!" he then turned back around to the Tahoe, swinging the golf club down against the side view mirror. Each whack of the golf club caused the side view mirror to break further and further.

"Leave my fucking truck alone!" the muscular man rushed Yung and grabbed the golf club. The men tussled over the golf club, trying to take it from one another. Suddenly, Yung kneed the buff dude in the nuts, causing his eyes to bug and cross. The hulking man doubled over grabbing his crotch in agony. His face was a dark pink and the veins in his forehead and neck swelled.

Yung whacked the muscular man in the ankle. He hollered aloud and grabbed his ankle, falling to the ground. He screamed in pain and threw up his arm to block Yung's assault. The little bastard was striking him over and over again, with the golf club. He had completely lost it. There was madness in his eyes and he was swinging the golf club with all of his might.

"Freeze!" a commanding voice yelled.

Yung's head snapped in the direction the authoritative voice came from. At the end of his line of vision, he saw three cops with their guns pointed at him. They wore dangerous expressions on their faces, and their trigger fingers were itching.

Yung froze in the place, holding the golf club back in a swinging position. One of the officers told him to drop his weapon and he obliged him. He then listened carefully to what the commanding officer told him to do. With the order having been given, Yung interlocked his fingers behind his head and got down on his knees. He stared straight ahead at nothing in particular, wearing a slight smirk on his lips.

A few days later, Yung winded up in Men's Central county jail with Bumpy. He watched the pint sized gangsta for an entire week, observing his daily routine and the company he kept. He hung around a clique of young wolves that worshipped him like a God, and were just as 'bout it' as he was. They followed him around like he was the president and they were secret service agents or some shit. There wasn't a nigga that could get close to him without one of the young bulls, pressing their line. Acknowledging this, Yung knew he was going to have to grease a few palms if he was going to be able to get close enough to Bumpy, to do what he'd been hired to do.

Yung got a few correctional officers into pocket that aided him in his mission. During a raid they planted a shank in Bumpy's cell. The violation sent Bumpy's black ass straight to the segregation unit, where unruly inmates were housed. Later that same night, Yung was taken from out of his cell and escorted to the segregation unit. Once he was there, the correctional officers removed his restraints. One of them handed him a syringe and a small glass bottle, that looked like its contents was insulin.

"Yeah, this is the right stuff?" Yung said as he read the label on the small bottle.

"Follow me." one of the two of the correctional officers motioned for Yung to follow him, as he headed towards the cell that housed Bumpy.

Yung walked behind the correctional officer, leaving the other officer down the corridor to keep an eye on things. As Yung followed behind the C.O, he shook up the small bottle and stuck the needle inside of it, drawing its contents inside of the syringe. Once the syringe was full, he stashed the bottle inside of the pocket. He then squirted some of the fluid out of the tip of the needle, as he held it before his eyes. A devilish smile curled both ends of his lips and his eyes glazed over with evil intent. While walking behind the correctional officer, Yung heard Bumpy hollering out shit from his cell.

"Limmie outta these fucking cuffs, man! Limmie the fuck go!" Yung heard Bumpy call out from his cell. "I swear 'fore God, when I get loose, that's y'all asses, man!"

"Yeah, yeah, yeah, just shut the fuck up!" Yung heard a different voice from Bumpy's cell. He figured it was one of the correctional officers, because someone had to be holding Bumpy down while the other officers retrieved him from his cell back in general population. Yung then heard Bumpy make a pained sound, so he gathered he'd been struck with either a fist or a blunt object.

"Real tough, real fucking tough, to hit a nigga with his hands and shit bound. Bitch ass nigga, limmie up so I can see what chu punk ass can do from the shoulders!"

"Didn't I tell you to shut the fuck up?" the correctional officer shouted. Afterwards, Yung heard more pained sounds from Bumpy as he was getting the shit beat out of him.

When Yung entered Bumpy's cell, he found two correctional officers holding the little gangsta down on his bunk. The nigga was talking mad shit and struggling to break free from the C.O's strong arms, but his efforts were useless. Once Bumpy saw the short Asian man at the door, he stopped bucking and looked him dead in his eyes, wondering who the hell he was.

"What the fuck is this, man? Who is this tight eyed mothafucka?" Bumpy asked, looking between the two correctional officers.

"Shhhhhhh." Yung advanced in Bumpy's direction, with his finger against his lips, shushing him. Using his other hand, he reached inside of his pocket and pulled out a handful of acupuncture needles.

"Limmie go, man, limmie go!" Bumpy fought to break free of the correctional officers.

"I'm tired of your shit!" one of the correctional officers holding down Bumpy said, frowning. He stood up and whipped out his Billy club, knocking Bumpy upside the head and in the chest. The little nigga threw up his free arm to shield himself, and the club left his limbs throbbing red.

"Bitch ass nigga!" the correctional officer stood over Bumpy, red faced and breathing heavily. His nostrils flared as his chest jumped up and down, as he breathed.

"I got it from here, step aside." Yung approached Bumpy as the correctional officers moved out of his way, leaving him a clear path to his victim. He approached the pint sized gangsta as he winced. Sitting down next to Bumpy, Yung stuck the needles in specific pressure points of his body, which left him paralyzed from the next down. Bumpy's eyes were big and his mouth was hanging open, as he tried moving from side to side. He wore a shocked expression on his face, and he couldn't believe what was happening to him.

"What the-what the fuck did you do to me, man?" A panic look crossed Bumpy's face. His eyes were full of fear, and Yung could see himself in his pupils.

"Don't worry; soon, all of this will be over. I promise." Yung stuck the last two needles in Bumpy's neck,

94

which stopped him from moving his mouth. The motha-fucka could no longer talk. "You know, your employer, Big Meat, has a great deal of love for you. When he hired me, he made my partner promise him that I'd make your death quick and as painless as possible." He took the pillow from behind Bumpy's head and held it with both hands. "He told my partner to have me tell you that this is business, nothing personal. He couldn't take a chance on you keeping your mouth shut, so he had to take precautions." With that having been said, Yung mashed the pillow over Bumpy's face until he believed he was dead. When he finally removed the pillow from off his victim's face, he had vacant eyes and a wide open mouth.

Once Yung had finished the job he was paid to do, he sat the pillow aside and flushed the needles down the toilet. Afterwards, he entered the corridor so that the correctional officer that had brought him down could shackle him up and take him back to his cell.

A few days later, Yung disappeared from out of the county jail, never to be seen again.

The next night

Flocka twisted the dials and shut off the hot shower water. He then stepped out of the tub and snatched a towel off the rack. He dried himself off and wrapped the towel around his waist, heading into his bedroom. He pulled out the top nightstand's drawer to grab a pair of boxer briefs and an undershirt when something at the corner of the mirror caught his eye. A small crinkle appeared on his forehead as he reached for the wallet size photo of him and Menace when they were teenagers. They were posted up on the side of their big homie's red Tahoe truck flamed up and pointing guns at whomever had taken the picture.

95

They were young, wild and reckless back then, and willing to do whatever they had to do to earn a name for themselves in the streets. They'd done most of their gangsta shit together, developing a brotherly bond and earning their peers admiration and respect.

Flocka plucked the photo from where it was wedged at the corner of the mirror and brought it closer to his eyes. A smirk spread at the corner of his lips remembering way back then.

Damn, Blood, we been through everything two YG's can go through together in the hood. My nigga Menace was the realist and truest friend a nigga ever had. He proved to be a standup nigga time and time again. And what the fuck did my snake ass do to my dawg? I betrayed 'em! Stabbed 'em right in his fuckin' back when all he ever did was show a nigga love! Flocka thought as his eyebrows arched and his nose wrinkled. Feeling ashamed of his actions, he shook his head and dropped the photo. He then balled his hand into a fist and thick veins formed on it. He clenched his jaws so tight that a thick vein bulged at his temple. His entire form trembled with anger and he suddenly launched his fist at the nightstand's mirror. The mirror's glass cracked into a cobweb and he pulled his fist back, blood trickling from his knuckles as they hung at his side. Quickly, he searched the drawers of his nightstand until he came up with a red bandana. He dabbed the bloody cuts in his hand with it and then tied it around his fist, flexing his fingers. Afterwards, he picked up the photo of him and Menace, staring down at his former homeboy's scowling face.

"I'ma make this shit right, Blood. Tonight. I put that on alla dead homies." Flocka swore and set the photo down on the nightstand. He then got dressed in all black, grabbed another red bandana and lifted his mattress, picking up the AK-47 he'd tucked there. Once he checked the banana clip of the choppa, he smacked it back into its belly and cocked that mothafucka. Afterwards, he wrapped it up in a blanket and headed out of the house.

****

It was well past midnight and The Drunken Monkey was closing. Mohamed had picked up the last chair and sat it upside down on a nearby table, when the last bar-maid came walking out of the back, tying her coat around her waist.

"Alright, Mo, I'm getting out of here now, come let me out." The barmaid said as she walked around the bar, heading towards the exit door.

Mohamed walked toward the door the same time as his co-worker, fishing around in his pocket for his keys. He pulled them out as soon as he reached the door; he unlocked the door and removed the latch that resided above and below the door. Afterwards, he pulled the door open and bid his coworker a farewell. Once he'd let her out, he went to shut the door behind her and a sneaker stepped in the doorway, stopping the door from closing. When he looked up, he met the serious eyes of a man wearing a red bandana over the lower half of his face. Mohamed's eyes bulged and his mouth dropped open in shock. He opened the door all the way up and homeboy rocking the red bandana shoved an AK-47 inside of his grill. The nigga then walked him back inside of the bar as he held his hands up in surrender.

"You do what I say, when I say it, or I'ma knock yo' head offa yo' shoulders with this big bitch, you under-stand me?" the man wearing the bandana spoke with a dead serious ass tone, letting Mohamed's ass know he wasn't there to play games.

"Uhn huh," Mohamed said as he nodded. He gagged and tears ran from the corners of his eyes, feeling old boy force his choppa further inside of his mouth piece.

"Good. Now, is Raffy still here?" Homeboy behind the bandana questioned.

Mohamed nodded, yes.

"Who else is up in here?" he looked around to see if he saw anybody in the area. Old boy didn't see anybody, so he focused his attention back on Mohamed. "It's just y'all two? Keep in mind, if you lie, I'ma knock yo' shit clean off yo' shoulders. Okay, now answer me."

Mohamed nodded, yes.

"Alright, I'ma take Big Daddy out cha mouth." he referred to his AK. "I want chu to lock this place up, then you and I are gonna go see yo' bitch ass brotha. Got it?"

Mohamed nodded his understanding. Homeboy took the AK out of his mouth and pointed it to the back of his dome, watching him lock up the bar. Once he was done, the man pressed the choppa to the back of his head again and walked him towards Raffy's office. They made their way upstairs, where the man looked up at the surveillance camera pointed down at them.

"Open this fuckin' doe right now, 'fore I leave this nigga's brains splattered on these walls! I know you know I'm out here and you can see me! I won't be askin' twice, homeboy! Fuck with me if you want to, and I'ma show you some gangsta shit you thought you could only see on TV! That's on everything I love!"

There was a buzzing sound and the black iron door clicked open. The man rocking the bandana told Mohamed to open both doors. Once he did, they made their way inside of Raffy's office. They found Raffy behind his desk with his hands raised in the air, mad dogging home-boy with the choppa to his brother's head.

"Do you know who I am, my friend?" Raffy asked, clenching his teeth. The vein at his temple throbbed angrily.

"Sho' you right. That's why I'm robbin' yo' motha-fuckin' ass! Now get over here at the center of the floor, and if you make any sudden moves, I'm painting the walls, ceiling and floors with you and this nigga'z blood. Now, hurry that ass up!" Raffy walked to the center of the office just like the man behind the bandana had or-dered. "Okay, now, spin around in a circle, then give yo' self a thorough pat down!" Raffy did as he was told. "Alright now, where the money at?"

"There's no money up here," Raffy let the lie roll off of his tongue. "Everything is downstairs in the register. Help yo' self!"

The dude holding Mohamed at gunpoint, tilted his head aside and looked at him like he couldn't believe he just said that. Right after, he shot Mohamed in the foot. The wounded man dropped to the floor and clutched his bleeding foot with both hands.

"Aaaaah! Aaaaah! Aaaah!" Mohamed screamed hys-terically louder and louder. As he held his foot, blood poured over his hands and slicked them wet.

"What the fuck did you do that for?" Raffy clenched his jaws and his nostrils flared. He looked like he wanted to beat that nigga with the AK ass, but he put himself in check. He knew that the wrong move would prove to be fatal for him. Old boy was strapped with so the scale was tilted in his favor.

"'Fore I came through that door," the man pointed to the door with his AK. "I told yo' ass to play with me if you want to! Now, where the fuck the money at? I'm talkin' 'bout them big dollas, I know you holdin'. You Arab niggaz be havin' that oil money, right? So come up off that!"

Raffy stared homeboy down hard, gritting his teeth. He didn't want to come up off the dead faces he had on lock, but he didn't want his brother getting smoked either. He loved his brother with all of heart, but he was stubborn as a mothafucka. He'd hate to take an L, and look like a sucker.

"Fuck. You." Raffy told him.

The nigga rocking the bandana shrugged and shot Mohamed's left ear off. Mohamed snapped his head back and his eyes looked like they were going to leap out of their sockets. He grabbed the area where his ear should have been and his hands came away bloody. He looked to his trembling bloody hand, screaming his head off. His voice rose several octaves.

"Aaaaaah! Aaaaaah! Aaaaaah!" Mohamed screamed in excruciation.

Out of the blue, he was silenced, when homeboy wearing the bandana cracked him across the back of the skull with the stock of his AK-47. He then pressed his sneaker against his chest as he lay unconscious and pointed the choppa at his face.

"Say goodbye to yo' brotha, my nigga!" old boy rocking the bandana told Raffy. He looked at him to see if he was going to fold and give him that paper he had on lock. When Raffy continued to mad dog him, and didn't say jack shit about breaking bread, homeboy moved to splatter Mohamed's shit.

100

"Okay, okay, okay, okay," A wide eyed Raffy outstretched his hands, trying to stop homeboy from smoking his brother. Seeing that the Arab had bowed down to his gangsta made the nigga with the AK-47 smile evilly, licking his gold teeth.

Bitch ass nigga, I knew yo' ass would fold!

Dude took the AK-47 from out of Mohamed's face and pointed it at Raffy. "Alright, now, get me that bag, I ain't got all night."

Raffy pulled open his bottom desk drawer and pulled out a duffle bag, sitting it on the desk top. He then removed the expensive painting from off his wall and revealed a safe. He opened the safe, revealing shelves of money in neat stacks, tangled in rubber bands. The Arab started snatching the stacks of out of the safe and tossing them inside of the duffle bag, talking shit as loaded it up.

"Yeaaaah, that's what I'm talkin' 'bout! Break mine off!" the dude nodded his head as he watched Raffy load the blue face bills inside of the duffle bag. He kept his eyes on him as he cleared out the safe and closed it back.

Once Raffy had finished loaded up the duffle bag, he zipped it up and walked it over to the nigga with the AK-47. Soon as dude hoisted the strap over his shoulder, he cocked his AK-47 over his shoulder and slammed it into Raffy's face, bloodying his nose. The Arab went cock eyed and fell backwards, crashing to the floor. He lay on his back, staring up at the ceiling, seeing shit out of focus. The nigga with the AK walked up on him. Looking down at him, he pointed the deadly end of his choppa at his grill. He then tilted his head to the side, appearing as if he was contemplating bodying Raffy or not.

"Uhhhh!"

The nigga with the AK-47 looked to Mohamed when he heard him moaning in pain on the floor. At that moment, Raffy noticed the tattoo on his neck which were prayer hands: *Only God can judge me* was over the hands. He was familiar with the ink. It was then that he knew who the man was robbing him, and he promised to God Almighty that if he lived through the night, he'd hunt him down and slaughter him.

Hearing police sirens heading to his location, the man wearing the bandana ran out of the office and down the staircase.

"I'm going to kill you, you hear me, Flocka? You black bastard! I'm going to kill you!" Raffy claimed as he continued to stare up at the ceiling. He was dizzy, and the lower half of his face was bloody. "You're dead, Flockaaaaaa!"

Chapter Six

Flocka hauled ass out of The Drunken Monkey. He bent the corner at the end of the block and didn't stop running until he reached his getaway car. As soon as he hopped in, he threw the duffle bag into the backseat, pulled the bandana down around his neck and fired up the vehicle. He busted a bitch, a U-turn, in the middle of the street going in the opposite direction. Hearing the police sirens nearby, he adjusted the rearview mirror and saw four police cars racing past the end of the block, where he'd turned the corner running. He then sighed with relief and lay back in his seat. He cruised through the residential street until he found a gutter where he could ditch the AK-47 he'd used in the kick door, the robbery. As soon as he spotted one, he hopped out of the getaway car with the choppa. He looked up and down the block to make sure no one was watching him. Once he saw that there wasn't any nosey mothafuckaz out, he threw the AK-47 down into the gutter. He then ran back to the car and hopped in behind the wheel. Next, he shut the door, shifted the gears and pulled off. As he drove through the streets, Flocka pulled out his cellular and speed dialed Menace. The nigga'z cell phone rung five times before he picked up.

****

Menace and Shatira were pillow fighting in their hotel room, when his cellular rang and vibrated.

"Okay, stop! I needa answer my jack." Menace said, smiling and breathing hard. He'd just gotten clobbered over the head by Shatira.

"Alright, nigga, but cho ass bet not try nothing." Shatira replied, breathing heavily and holding her pillow at her side. A smile was on her face.

"I'm not, man, chill yo' lil' ass out." He chuckled. He then faked like he was going to walk away and clobbered her ass with his pillow. The blow knocked her back on the bed, giggling and laughing.

"I knew your old slick ass was gon' try something, nigga." Shatira said from where she was lying on her back, halfway off of the bed.

Menace tossed the pillow on her face and walked over to his cell phone which was on the dresser. He picked his cellular up. Once he saw that it was Flocka hitting him up, his face balled up in hatred. By this time, Shatira had smacked the pillow off her face and sat up in bed. Lines formed on her forehead as she wondered who it was calling that changed her man's mood.

"Who is that, babe?" Shatira inquired, rising from off the bed.

"Flocka!" Menace spat like his former friend's name left a bad taste in his mouth.

"Are you gonna answer it?"

Menace nodded and accepted the call. "'Sup, Blood?" he said into the receiver with a *What the fuck you want?* Attitude.

"'Sup, bro? Man, I know what chu thinkin'. And I ain't even on that time, dawg. I just called to apologize to you. We 'pose to be brothas, and I did some foul ass shit, gettin' you crossed up with this nigga Big Meat..." Flocka gave Menace the rundown on everything. By the time he finished, he was winded but he was glad he'd gotten everything off his chest.

"So, what's 'pose to happen now, bro? We still at one another's necks? If so, me and you can meet up where ever, whenever and settle this shit like G's."

"Nah. Like I told you, homeboy. I ain't even on that time. I got Meat's bread. I'm finna drop it off to 'em. I'ma tell 'em everything I just told you. The whole truth and nothin' but the truth. Whatever he chooses to do to me, I'ma take that shit like a G. You know what I'm sayin'?"

Menace was quiet for a second. "If you do it like that, he sho' 'nough gon' leave you stanking. You know how Blood get down for his."

"Yeah, I know. But I'ma man, and a man takes responsibility for his actions." Flocka told him.

"Respect."

"While I got chu on the jack, there's somethin' else I gotta get off my chest, my nigga."

Menace took a deep breath. For the life of him he couldn't figure out what else Flocka could have to drop on him. He wasn't sure if he could handle anything else. Shit, the nigga had already tried to pop him, and he found that hard to deal with, being that he was supposed to have been his main man and shit.

"Speak on it, Damu." Menace said into his cellular. At this time, Shatira was leaning her ear against the back of his cell phone trying to listen in on the conversation. Having grown tired of struggling to listen, she whispered to him to put the device on speaker phone.

Shatira stood right beside Menace waiting to hear exactly what Flocka had to say. There was silence for a minute as Flocka took the time to take a breath, like it was going to be really hard for him to say what was on his mind.

"Cee Cee and her people are dead." Flocka spat out.

"Oh, noooo." Shatira's eyes filled up with tears, instantly. She made an ugly face and smacked her hands over her mouth. She shook her head like she couldn't believe what she'd just heard. Seeing his woman hurt by the bad news, Menace pulled her into him, letting her bury her face into his chest.

Holding Shatira against him with one arm, Menace used the other to hold his cellular so he could finish listening to what Flocka had to say.

"How do you know this, Blood? What happened to 'em?" Menace inquired.

"That makes sense! That makes sense as to why she hasn't been answering my calls. I thought she was mad at me or something, but she was dead." Shatira said as she looked up at him, tears cascading down her cheeks. She sniffled and swallowed the lump of hurt in her throat.

Menace looked down at Shatira and nodded, letting her know she was right.

"Yo', bro, you still there?" Menace asked Flocka, wondering if he was still on the jack.

"Yeah, bro, I'm still here. And as far as lil' momma and her people...I know about that 'cause, well, take a wild guess." Flocka said.

Shatira's eyebrows arched and her nose scrunched up. She exchanged glances with Menace, and knew that they both were thinking the same thing. She then looked at the cellular he was holding in his hand.

"Wait a minute, are you tryna say you popped my best friend and her family?" Shatira asked. When Flocka didn't respond, she snatched the cell phone from out of Menace's hand and walked away with it, like she wanted time to talk with him privately. "Flocka, did you or did you not kill my sister and her family?" Again there was silence, which angered her further. "I know you hear me, you mothafucka! Be a man and 'fess up for what the fuck you did, you coward!" Menace went to take his cell phone from Shatira, but she pushed his hand away. She wasn't done with Flocka's ass yet.

"Yeah, I did it. That's what the fuck you wanna hear? Huh? We put the love on the whole mothafuckin' family! You happy now? Are you? Are you fuckin' happy?"

Shatira held the cellular to her bosom, silently crying. The tears coming from her eyes appeared to have drenched her face. She was in great eternal pain, and she didn't know what to do. The emotional hurt she was experiencing was damn near crippling her. She wiped her eyes with the back of her hand, sniffled and swallowed the spit in her throat.

Once Shatira had gotten herself together, she placed the cell phone back to her ear. She shut her eyelids briefly and took a breath, peeling her eyelids back open. She scowled and clenched her jaws, showcasing the skeletal bone structure in her face.

"You're a dead man, you hear me, nigga? You're a dead man walking! I don't know where you are, or who you're with! But once I catch up witchu, I'ma squash that ass! That's on my daddy and my mothafucking momma, bitch! Believe that!"

Right then, Flocka disconnected the call.

Shatira dropped her hand to her side and released the cell phone, letting it fall at her feet. She then turned around to Menace, tears dripping from the brims of her eyes, continuously. Her bottom lip quivered and her eyes misted with more tears. Seeing how fucked up she was emotionally, Menace hugged her, affectionately. He then kissed her on the side of her head and rubbed her back, trying his best to make her feel comforted.

Shatira pulled her face away from Menace's shirt. Looking up into his eyes, she said, "I want chu to take me where he lives, babe. I want this mothafucka bad. I want him so bad, my clits hard. He's gotta go, he's gotta go tonight."

As Menace stared down into Shatira's eyes, he wondered if he could go through with killing Flocka or not. Although the nigga had tried to pop his top, he still had mad love for him. He couldn't see himself putting a bullet in his head, but he knew that in order to prove his loyalty to Shatira he'd have to go along with helping her body him. There wasn't any way in hell he was going to choose the life of the man that had tried to murder him over his fiancée. Little momma was his ride or die, and no one came before her.

"Alright," Menace began, wiping her dripping eyes with his thumbs. "You wanna get this nigga, then let's get this nigga.

Shatira dapped him up. They then grabbed their guns, tucked them and left the hotel room.

****

After Flocka got off the jack with Menace and Shatira, he hit up Big Meat. The big man answered on the third ring.

"What's up?" Big Meat said.

"I needa kick it to you for a second, OG. You gotta few ticks for me?"

There was a moment of silence before Big Meat spoke again.

"Yeah, go head."

"I had somethin' to do with yo' bag gettin' taken. Matter fact, the whole shit was on me. I was into some towel heads for three hunnit large, and if I didn't pay 'em back, then they was gone dead my ass. My nigga Menace ain't have shit to do with it. In exchange for yo' money, I only ask that you spare him. However you choose to handle me is all on you. I'ma just take my punishment like a man." Flocka looked up at the rearview mirror, seeing his cheeks wet and the brims of his eyes red. The way he'd been crying you'd think he'd found out his momma just died, but that wasn't the case. He was so emotional because he'd done some scandalous ass shit to a nigga that was like a brother to him. In doing what he'd done he knew he'd broke his heart, and that was something he wasn't sure he'd be able to live with.

"Where are you now?" Big Meat asked.

Flocka couldn't read how Big Meat was feeling. He was expecting him to go the fuck off but he hadn't. His stomach growled and twisted in knots, as he wondered what his fate would be. The anticipation was killing him, but he knew he'd have to hold out if he was going to find out anything.

"I'm in traffic. What's up? You tryna link up? I can meet chu anywhere. The ball is in yo' court, big dawg."

"Meet me in that Super Buy parking lot over on Vermont Avenue…" Big Meat gave him the date and time to meet him.

"Alright. Super Buy parking lot at 10 o'clock. I got it. And listen, man, I'm sorry about all…" Flocka frowned up and looked at his cellular. Big Meat had hung up on his ass. "Fuck, Blood!" he threw his cell phone at the windshield and it deflected off of it, landing on the floor on the passenger side. "That's it, man. I'm dead! I'm dead! I may as well blow my own fuckin' brains out now." he gripped the steering wheel and banged his forehead against it. Afterwards, he leaned forward and pulled his gun from underneath the driver's seat. He cocked a live round into its head and shoved it inside of his grill, biting down on the cold steel and plastic. He squeezed his eyelids shut and breathed huskily, trying to pump himself up to blow his head off. Suddenly, he took the banga out of his mouth and lowered it at his side. "I can't...I can't do it. I gotta offa myself up so this nigga Meat will spare Menace." Flocka let down the passenger window and threw his gun out of it. He then fired up the getaway car, looked over to make sure there weren't any oncoming vehicles and pulled out into traffic. "Fuck it. It is what it is. If I get dealt with, then I get dealt with." Flocka said, sounding like Smokey from the movie, *Friday.*

****

Big Meat stood outside his Bentley smoking a Cuban cigar, smoke wafting around him and obscuring his face. There was an ear-bud in his ear. His head was on a swivel as he took in his surroundings, wondering when Flocka was going to come driving up. He blew smoke out of his mouth and pulled back his sleeve, displaying his Movado watch. Once he glanced at the time, he lowered his arm at his side and continued puffing his cigar, blowing out smoke rings.

"Come on, cocksucka, show your face, so I can have my guys blow you away." Big Meat said to himself as he continued to indulge in his cigar. He glanced over his right and left shoulder, seeing his killaz lurking in the shadows with AK-47s. He gave the head killa a nod and he returned the gesture. He then focused his attention on the traffic outside of the parking lot, looking for Flocka to pull up any minute then.

There wasn't any way that Big Meat was letting Flocka slide after the shit he pulled. No one stole from him and gets to see another sun rise. That mothafucka had to die, and tonight was the night. As soon as he got his money back from him, he was going to walk off and give his hittaz the code word to move in and lay his ass out. He had a total of six niggaz with choppas equipped with one-hundred round drums and infrared lasers, lying in the cut ready to light Flocka's monkey ass up.

A smile stretched across Big Meat's face as soon as he saw Flocka walking up, duffle bag in hand.

"Here his lil' bitch ass comes now." Big Meat said to his killaz through his ear-bud. He then converted his jovial expression to a stern one once Flocka pulled up and parked. He threw open his door, slammed it shut and walked to the back door. He opened the back door and took out the duffle bag, slamming the door behind him. Flocka made his way over to Big Meat with a confident stride, keeping eye contact with him along the way. Although his face was stern, his heart was thudding. He was just waiting for a nigga to jump out of the shadows and knock his head off. In fact, he was low key; looking around to see if saw anyone lurking in the corners and cuts. He didn't see anyone, but even if he had, he wouldn't have ran. He was just going to let the shit go down. He would face his fate on his feet, head held high, like a mothafucking man.

"'Sup, Big Meat?" Flocka raised his fist to dap him up. Big Meat just looked at him without saying a word, so he dropped his hand at his side.

Big Meat dropped the cigar at his dress shoe and mashed it out, smearing black and gray ashes. He then blew out the little smoke that was left in his mouth and said, "Is my money in that bag?" he pointed to the duffle bag that Flocka was holding at his side.

"Yeah." Flocka answered. Big Meat snatched the duffle bag out of his hand causing him to look at him like he was out of his fucking mind. He watched as the big man unzipped the bag and looked over its contents. It was full of dead presidents. Having confirmed this, Big Meat zipped the bag back up and hoisted its strap over his shoulder. The crime boss looked him dead in his eyes, jaws locked, eyes holding an intense gaze. "So, what happens now?" he shrugged.

Big Meat stepped forward causing Raffy to look uneasy. He cupped his face and kissed him on the forehead, saying, "That was The Kiss of Death!" He then shoved him and walked off towards his car. As soon as stepped off, his killaz spilled from out of the shadows with their AK-47s equipped with drums. They focused the red dots of their infrared lasers on Flocka. Flocka's eyes got as big as saucers and his mouth hung open. He looked around and gasped, seeing his would-be killaz closing in on him.

At that moment, police cars with their blue and red lights flashing, poured inside of the parking lot. The killaz and Big Meat looked around surprised. They didn't know what the fuck was going down. Before they knew it, the cops were jumping out of their cars, drawing handguns and shotguns on them. The killaz threw down their AK-47s and placed their hands behind their heads. Big Meat threw down the duffle bag and followed suit, doing exactly what was told to the killaz by the cops. Everyone then got down on their knees. Some of the cops moved in to handcuff them, while others kept their guns drawn on them in case they tried some shit.

****

Flocka managed to slip out of Super Buy's parking lot as the police cars rolled in. One of the cops spotted him and now he had a police car on his ass, flashing the spot light around the neighborhood as he ran. Flocka was sweaty, droplets dripping from the corner of his brow. He was huffing and puffing, constantly looking over his shoulder.

"Haa! Haa! Haa! Haa! Haa! Haa! Haa!" Flocka wiped his forehead with the back of his hand and kept on running. His chest was burning and his knees were killing him, but he'd rather die on his feet then have those metal bracelets around his wrists.

Flocka looked over his shoulder again. The police car had turned off its spot light and was now speeding in his direction. Acknowledging this, Flocka dove into a neighboring yard and crawled across the lawn. Reaching the side of the house, he got upon his knees and peered out of the yard into the street. Breathing heavily, Flocka watched as the police car turned around in someone's driveway and went back in the direction it came from.

Flocka looked down at the ground, with sweat still dripping from his brow. He breathed huskily as he crossed himself in the sign of the holy crucifix. "Thank you, God! Thank you."

Flocka stayed on the side of the house until he thought the police were gone. He then rose to his feet, took a deep breath to gather his wits and headed out of the yard. He caught the bus home.

****

Flocka made his way down the sidewalk toward his house. He unlatched the short gate and pushed it open, trekking his way through his yard. Coming upon the front porch, he fished his keys out of his pocket and unlocked the front door. He was about to push the door open, when he thought he heard something on the other side of the door. His brows wrinkled and he placed his ear to the door, listening closely. Once he didn't hear anything, he shrugged and walked inside of his house, over the threshold. He shut the door behind him and locked it, placing the chain on it. Afterwards, he journeyed inside of the kitchen and opened the refrigerator. He scanned the shelves until he found a carton of Donald Duck orange juice. He took out the carton of OJ and opened it, taking it to his head. His throat moved up and down as he drunk thirstily from the carton, spilling a little of its contents.

Flocka took the carton from his lips and wiped his mouth with the back of his fist. He then burped and made his way towards his bedroom.

"It's dark as a mothafucka in here, Blood." Flocka acknowledged how dark his home was as he made his way down the hallway. Reaching his bedroom, he tried flipping on the light switch, but the light wouldn't come on. His forehead crinkled and he walked over to the nightstand, trying to turn on the lamp. Once the lamp light didn't turn on, he picked up the remote control and tried turning on the flat screen. The television didn't turn on either. "Fuck is up? The power went out or some shit?"

Flocka tossed the remote control onto the bed and headed for the door. As soon as he reached it, he found Shatira standing before him with her gun pointed at him. His eyes doubled in size and his mouth dropped open.

Before he could say a fucking word, Shatira was pulling the trigger.

Blowl!

The bullet went through the carton of orange juice and struck Flocka in the shoulder. He hollered out and launched the carton at her. Shatira turned her head as the carton struck her in the head, spilling some of its contents. That split second was all the time Flocka needed to react. He yanked the cord of the lamp out of the wall and knocked her gun out of her hand with it, as it fired again. He then grabbed the lamp by both hands and slammed it down against her head. The lamp exploded and sent shards raining down upon the carpet. Shatira hit the carpeted floor hard, moaning in pain.

Flocka spared a glance at Shatira, before grabbing his bleeding shoulder and hauling ass to the front door. Swiftly, he unchained and unlocked the door. As soon as he pulled the mothafucka open, he came face to face with the barrel of Menace's gun. Although he was masked up, Flocka knew it was Menace pointing the banga at him. He could tell it was him by his posture and his eyes.

"Go ahead, my nigga, get this shit over with." Flocka told Menace as he lifted his hands up into the air. He stared him right in his eyes as he waited for him to deliver the kill-shot.

Menace didn't say anything as he stared his former friend in the face. He tried to decide whether he should kill him or not. Menace knew this was what Shatira wanted, but he wasn't for sure if he could live the rest of his life knowing he was the one behind his homeboy's murder or not. Out of all of the dirt he'd done in the streets, he wasn't sure if he could go throughout his life with Flocka's body on his conscience.

Menace's eyes looked to the left of Flocka. He saw Shatira moaning as she slowly tried to get to her feet.

"Get outta here, now." Menace told him in a hushed tone so that Shatira wouldn't hear him.

Flocka frowned and said, "So, you can pop me in my back? Fuck that! If you gon' do me then do me while I'm facin' you, like a mothafuckin' man."

Menace scowled and spoke through clenched teeth, "My nigga, if you don't get cho ass outta here, I'ma shoot chu dead in yo' face, so help me God I'll peel yo' cap."

Flocka stared Menace down for a second, trying to read him. He was trying to figure out if he was being deceitful or not. As far as he could tell, the young nigga was keeping it one-hundred with him.

Abruptly, Flocka took off running off the front porch. He reached the sidewalk and ran as fast as he could, holding his wounded shoulder.

Menace looked at him run until he was swallowed up by the night. He then turned around to Shatira, she was still dizzy trying to get back upon her feet.

"Okay, here goes nothing," Menace said under his breath. He then gripped his gun with both hands and bumped around on the porch, pretending to be fighting over control of the banga. He fired off a shot into the air, and then flung his gun across the front lawn. Next, he punched himself in the stomach which caused him to double over. He followed up by socking himself in both jaws and landed a punch flush in the face. The blow knocked his head backwards and sent him sliding down the steps, landing on the concrete. He lay there on his back, moaning in pain with a small stream of blood running out of the corner of his mouth.

At that moment, Shatira ran out of the house clutching her gun with both hands. Her neck was on a swivel, as she looked around for any threat to her and Menace's lives. When she didn't see anyone, she lowered her gun at her side and cautiously walked over to Menace. Kneeling down, she felt under his shirt to see if he had any gunshot wounds. He didn't have any.

"Baby, are you, okay?" Shatira asked concerned, looking around for Flocka.

"Uuhhhh." Menace sat up, rubbing the back of his head. He winced as he went on to talk. "I'll be straight. Homeboy gotta 'way though."

"Fuck!" Shatira said as she stood upright and tucked her banga at the small of her back. She then pulled Menace up to his feet.

"My bad, babe." Menace apologized.

"Don't worry about it. We'll catch up with dude one day." Shatira assured Menace as she rubbed the side of his face, lovingly.

Menace searched the lawn until he recovered his gun. He then grabbed Shatira's hand and fled the yard. Far off in the distance, they could hear Twelve approaching, hastily.

****

Menace and Shatira walked down the corridor toward their hotel room, holding hands. A frown crept upon Menace's face as he saw a man approaching. He was wearing a baseball cap and a hoodie and his hands were inside of his pockets. As Menace neared the man, he tilted his head downward to avoid eye contact.

"Yo', you peeped that?" A creased brow Menace asked Shatira.

"Yeah, babe, that nigga looked suspect. Where you think he was coming from?" Shatira inquired, looking over her shoulder. When she looked, she saw the man glance in their direction before ducking off inside of the elevator that had just arrived.

"I don't know, but chu open the door. I'ma hold us down." Menace told his girl as he stuck his hand underneath his shirt for his banga. He stood at the back of Shatira, looking up and down the hallway as she pulled out her key-card to open the door.

Shatira stuck the key-card into the door mechanism and the red light on it turned green. The device beeped and she turned the handle, pushing her way inside of the bedroom.

****

When Ducey emerged from out of the hotel, he looked over his shoulder at the same floor he'd just left from. He knew right then that Menace and Shatira were viewing the recording that Fonzell had him leave behind. He found great satisfaction in knowing he'd carried out his running partner's last wishes. He felt a sense of accomplishment, and sadness at the same time. Before he knew it, his eyes formed with water and obscured his vision. Big teardrops fell from his lower eyelids and slashed on the ground, some hitting the tip of his sneaker.

Ducey wiped his eyes with the sleeve of his shirt as he walked across the hotel's parking lot. Seeing a yellow taxi cab pulling inside the parking lot, he waved it down. The vehicle slowed to a stop and he hopped into the backseat.

"Where to, my friend?" the Indian driver asked, glancing up at Ducey through the rearview mirror. He could tell by his glassy, pink eyes that he'd been crying. Old

Ducey looked kind of shady to him, but he didn't give a fuck. He needed his fare. He had a wife and five kids to provide for, so he was trying to snatch every dollar he could get his hands on. Besides, he rode with a .32 handgun, just in case any passengers he picked up wanted to kick up so shit.

"Ummm, uh," Ducey thought on it for a second. He was sitting in the backseat of the cab staring at a packet of dope he'd purchased on his way over to the hotel. He'd gotten it into his mind that he was going to get high to wash away the pain that Fonzell's death had brought him. But right then he couldn't help thinking about the promise he'd made to his friend to get clean once he was gone. Fonzell had even gave him a bankroll to tie him over once he'd finished his stint at the Matrix Institute, which was a rehabilitation center out in Rancho Cucamonga.

"Buddy, where are you going? I don't have all night, ya know?" the Indian driver glanced up at Ducey again through the rearview mirror. He could tell that his attention was focused down on something but he didn't know what.

Ducey continued to stare down at the packet of dope in his palm, trying to make up his mind on what he should do. Having finally came to the conclusion of what he was going to do, he held down the button that descended the back passenger window and threw out the packet. Afterwards, he let the window back up and wiped the moisture from his eyes with his thumb.

"The Matrix Institute out in Rancho Cucamonga. The address is..." Ducey went on to give the driver the address to the rehabilitation center. He then laid back in the seat and stared out of the back window, watching the streets whip past him.

119

"You okay back there, my friend?" the driver inquired. He could feel something was bothering Ducey, and was trying to get it out of him. He was use to his passengers engaging him in conversation. He'd grown quite use to it, too. Most of time when he started chopping it up with someone he'd picked up, the ride would go by within the time it took a mothafucka to snap his fingers.

"I'm straight. Wake me up once we get there." Ducey pulled his baseball cap low over his brows. He then adjusted himself in the seat and bowed his head, folding his arms across his chest.

"You got it." the driver replied.

The taxi was quiet. In fact, it was so quiet that it was driving the Indian driver crazy. He had to say something in hopes of sparking a conversation with Ducey.

The Indian driver adjusted the rearview mirror so he could get a better look at Ducey as he addressed him. "My friend, what do you think about that Laker game last..."

The words died in the driver's throat when he saw Ducey was fast asleep, snoring. Having acknowledged this, the driver shrugged and turned the volume up on a talk radio station.

****

When Menace and Shatira came through the door of their hotel room they found a camcorder sitting on top of a letter. Instantly, their foreheads crinkled and they wondered who'd been inside of their room. Menace pulled out his banga so did Shatira. They checked the room thoroughly, before finding themselves at the bed the camcorder was lying on.

"Who do you think left it?" Shatira asked with a creased brow, picking up the letter.

"I don't know, but my money is on that shady looking nigga that past us in the hallway." Menace told her as he picked up the camcorder. Wonderment creased his forehead once he saw a sticky-note attached to the side of the recording device. He hadn't noticed it until he'd picked the cam up. "Play me. Do not read the letter 'til I tell you to in the video." he read the sticky-note which he'd plucked off the side of the camcorder. Shatira looked over at the sticky-note, lip reading it as he held in his hand.

Menace took a deep breath and walked around the bed, sitting beside Shatira so they could view the footage together. Menace opened the camcorder and pressed the play button on it. Instantly, Fonzell popped up on the small screen.

"Hey, son." Fonzell greeted his offspring. "Unfortunately, if you're viewing this, I'm dead. Let me say I'm truly, truly sorry. I'm partially responsible for the hurt you're experiencing right now. And I'm willing to accept that, 'cause what I did was outta love for you. So, you can bet your ass I'd do it again...in a heartbeat."

Menace's eyes welled up with tears and he bit down hard on his bottom lip. Shatira looked up at him and felt bad, she hated to see her man grieving. She wiped away his tears as soon as they spilled down his cheeks, and kissed him on the side of his face. Afterwards, she hooked her arm in his arm and leaned her head against his shoulder, watching his father on the screen.

"Tonight, a DVD of my death by Big Meat's hands will be delivered to 77th street precinct. I did this for not only you and myself, but for the love of my life, your darling mother..." Fonzell took a deep breath as tears filled his eyes. The teardrops fell one after another and he wiped them away with his curled finger. He then blinked back the moisture in his eyes. "There's something else I'd like to tell you...something that may change the way you feel, and look at me and your mother, but I'm going to tell you anyway. I'm going to tell you 'cause it's your right to know." Fonzell looked up at the ceiling and mouthed something that only the Lord could hear. Bringing his head back down, he looked directly into the camera's lens. "As you already know, Big Meat and I were best friends growing up. What you didn't know was your mother was his wife long before she and I got together. In fact, she started seeing me behind his back." Menace and Shatira exchanged glances with this revelation having been revealed. They then focused their attention back on the small screen of the camcorder. "I know that sounds fucked up, but it is what it is. Anyway, let's get into the meat and potatoes of this story..."

A sweaty Fonzell chopped logs with an axe as his body dripped with perspiration. He was wearing tight blue jeans and snake skin cowboy boots. His face was balled up and his jaws were clenched. He'd hoist his axe high above his head and swing it downward into the log, splitting it into halves. As soon as the halves would split, he'd grab another one of the short logs and place it down on the stump. He'd chop that one in two and continue the process. Once he'd made himself a nice pile of firewood, he sat the axe aside and pulled off his gloves. After he tucked the gloves into his back pocket, he wiped his beaded forehead with the back of his hand and picked up his canteen. Screwing the top off of the canteen, he then took it to his mouth, guzzling it, thirstily. Once he'd quenched his thirst, he screwed the top back onto it. Hearing someone driving up at his back, he turned around to find a black Escalade truck with black tinted windows you'd have to have X-ray vision to see through.

The enormous truck stopped and some goons jumped out, followed by a large black man. He was tall and as dark as the tar used to slick rooftops with. He was smoking a cigar and wearing a snazzy suit. The suit made him look more like a Wall Street broker than the crime boss he actually was and that was quite all right with him. The tall dark-skinned man in the debonair suit name was Big Meat.

Big Meat spat his half smoked cigar to the ground and removed his suit's jacket, laying it across the hood of his truck. He then unbuttoned the cuffs of his dress shirt and rolled up his sleeves. Next, he snatched the axe out of the stump as he advanced in Fonzell's direction, telling his goons, "Hold his right hand down on that stump over there!"

Fonzell's brows lowered and he threw up his fists. He looked around at the goons as they were approaching him. "Come on! Come on, you mothafuckaz!"

Fonzell put up a fight, but he wasn't a match for the four men that had been sent to restrain him. When he showed resistance, they punched and kicked him until he was too battered and weakened to put up a fight. His eyes rolled to their whites and he moaned in pain. Fonzell couldn't do anything as one of them out stretched his hand over the stump. Hearing someone at his left, he looked up and saw two blurred Big Meat's in front of him. Slowly, his vision came into focus and he saw one Big Meat coming at him, with an axe.

Fonzell looked up at Big Meat with big eyes as he stood over him with the axe. The big man mad dogged him and hoisted the axe over his head. Grunting, he swung the axe downward and it whistled through the air. The axe sliced through Fonzell's wrist bone and stabbed into the tree stump. Fonzell's eye's nearly popped out of his head and he screamed bloody murder.

"Aaaaaaaaaah!" Fonzell threw his head back as he screamed, displaying all of the cavities inside of his mouth. The veins became pronounced in his forehead and neck. He took his stump from off the tree stump as it squirted blood, looking at it in shock. Suddenly, his eyes rolled to their whites and he collapsed to the ground.

"You were 'pose to be my best friend, and you do me like this? Fuck you!" Big Meat harped up a glob of phlegm and spit in Fonzell's face.

"He's going into shock!" one of the goons informed Big Meat.

"Hold his ass still and outstretch his stump!" Big Meat snatched the axe out of the tree stump. He then held it's blade in the flames of a nearby campfire until it turned ember. Having done this, he walked over to Fonzell where he was being held. Carefully, he pressed the axe's ember blade against Fonzell's bloody stump. Instantly, his eyes snapped open in bearable pain.

"Aaaahhhh!" Fonzell threw his head back and hollered out, feeling the blade against his flesh. When Big Meat took his axe away from his stump it wafted with smoke. The end of the stump was now black and was no longer bleeding.

"Toss this piece of shit in the truck." Big Meat ordered Bumpy and his goons. They didn't waste any time duct taping a moaning Fonzell up and dragging his ass across the ground toward the hatch of the Escalade truck. They tossed him into the back of the SUV and slammed the hatch shut. They then smacked the dirt from their *hands and joined back up with Big Meat. Once they were by the big man's side, he looked up to the cabin, and said, "Y'all go grab that bitch!"*

"We on it, boss dawg. Y'all niggaz come on." Bumpy motioned for the goons to follow him as he charged up the stairs of the cabin. He snatched open the door and they stormed inside. Right after, a lot of racket was going on inside of the cabin. Moochie was screaming and hollering, dishes were shattering on the floor, and furniture was being toppled over. After a while, the racket stopped. The only voice Big Meat heard was Moochie's, as he reached into the small of his back and pulled out a black leather case, heading up the steps of the cabin.

"Limmie go, limmie go gotdammit!" Moochie screamed at the top of her lungs.

Big Meat entered the cabin and went straight to the kitchen. Looking upon the floor, he saw his goons holding Moochie down to the floor. She struggled to get away from them, but her efforts were useless, the men were just too strong for her.

"I knew I'd find yo' trifling, no good ass here, you disloyal ass bitch!" Big Meat mad dogged her, as hatred bled from his eyes. "When I found you, you weren't shit, a goddamn dope fiend. I took a chance on you, cleaned you up, gotchu into rehab, gave you a life better than the one you had. And what the fuck do you to repay me, huh? You fuck my best friend behind my back, and make me look like a fucking chump in the streets. But that's okay. That's quite okay. 'Cause payback's a coldhearted mothafucka, and his name is Big Meat."

Big Meat walked over to the kitchen table and unzipped the black leather case. Inside there was a packet of dope, a syringe, cotton balls and a couple of other items used to shoot heroin with. The big man didn't waste any time preparing a shot of dope, ignoring everything Moochie had to say as he did so.

"Oh, my God, please, Meat, don't do this, don't do this to me!" Moochie's eyes filled with tears, as she watched her husband prepare a syringe of dope for her. "If you give me that shit, I'ma relapse and be back on dope again! It took me forever to kick that shit, Meat! Pleeeease, I'm begging you, don't do this to me!" Moochie's face balled up as she struggled to get free of the goons grasps again, but they held fast.

Big Meat whipped around, face fixed with a frightening scowl, saying, "Don't do this to you? Do this to you? Bitch, what about what chu did to me, huh? You ever thought about that shit? Have you?"

The big man's eyes threatened to drip tears, but he blinked them back. He couldn't have his goons seeing him vulnerable. He had to remain a gangsta at all times in front of them. With that in mind, he turned back around to finish up with the heroin. He'd just stuck the needle into the swollen piece of cotton ball in the spoon which had absorbed the dope he'd been cooking in it.

"I'm sorry, Meat, I'm sorry! I swear to God, I'm sorry!" Moochie whimpered. Tears bursts through her eyes and ran down her cheeks. "Think about our baby, think about him!"

"Fuck that lil' nigga, he probably not mine, anyway," He told her over his shoulder, and then went back to drawing the heroin into the syringe. A couple of seconds later, he turned around with the syringe, looking upon it in awe. He thumped the syringe's shaft and squirted some of the dope out of the tip of its needle. Big Meat's lips curled at both ends and an evil smile stretched across his

face. "*Yeah, I hear yo' cries for help and shit, but love don't live here no more, bitch! That shit died the day you letta 'notha nigga run up in what was 'pose to be mine, forever. And you ain't just let some nigga from across town hit it. Nah, yo' foul ass let my main-mothafucking-man, my brotha from anotha smash! Fuck some sympathy! I ain't got no remorse for yo' ho ass!*"

Big Meat stuck the syringe between his teeth and bit down on it. He then unbuckled his belt and pulled it free from the loops of his slacks. He continued to smile evilly as he slowly walked towards Moochie, taunting her in a way.

Moochie's eyes bulged and her mouth dropped open. Her heart thudded and she felt her bladder filling. Again, she tried to break free of Bumpy and the goons. They held onto her, but she damn near broke loose from them.

"*Hold her down, hold this bitch down!*" *Big Meat ordered his goons, still clutching the syringe between his teeth.*

Bumpy and two other goons struggled to hold Moochie down. She screamed and hollered, trying her best to break loose from their grasps. She winded up snatching her leg from out of Bumpy's hands and kicking him in the mouth, busting his grill. The little gangsta staggered backwards, holding his bleeding mouth. He caught his balance, and frowned up. Taking his hand away from his mouth, he saw that his palm was bloody. His eyebrows arched and he bit down on his inner jaw, balling his hands into fists.

"*Fuckin' whore!*" *an angry Bumpy cracked Moochie in the chin, dazing her. The blow left her moaning and her eyes rolled to their whites. She was vulnerable to Big Meat's will now, and not much of a threat to his goons.*

"Step aside." Big Meat ordered Bumpy. The little gangsta moved out of his path, poking at his bleeding wound with his tongue as he walked away.

Big Meat looped the belt around Moochie's arm and pulled it tight, buckling it. Afterwards, he searched the inside of her arm for a fat, juicy vein. As soon as he found it, he harped up some saliva and spat on it. Once he rubbed the spit onto her vein, he took the syringe out of his mouth and brought the needle near her vein.

Moochie's head snapped to her arm as Big Meat brought the needle towards it. Her eyes bucked and her mouth quivered. She was absolutely terrified. "Please, Meat, I'm sorry! I-mothafucking-apologize!"

"Fuck yo' apology, skeeza!" Big Meat spat hatefully as he pierced her pronounced vein with the syringe's needle. As soon as the needle penetrated her arm, Moochie hollered out and squinted her eyes. She saw her blood release inside the shaft of the syringe and tint the dope in it burgundy.

"Wait, wait, wait, wait! What did you expect for me to do, huh? You never let me leave the house, you beat me every time you had a fucked up day, you were never affectionate, and you never took me out anywhere! For Christ sake, I wasn't even sure if you loved me!" Moochie spat panicky. She knew that once she got hooked on dope again, she'd return to her old ways. The last thing she wanted was to be struggling to kick a habit again. It was hell! "Fonzell was right there, he gave me what chu didn't! He gave me love, affection, admiration, and, ahhhh!"

Big Meat pushed the plunger of the syringe and the dope rushed inside of Moochie's system. Her head dropped to the floor and her eyes rolled. Her mouth *stretched wide open. The bitch looked like she was being possessed by an evil spirit, but that couldn't have been further from the truth. The dope was taking effect, and she was feeling how she did the first time she indulged in the shit.*

Big Meat unbuckled the belt from Moochie's arm and pulled it loose. He capped the syringe and tossed it into the trash can. He stood up and slid his belt through the loops of his slacks, buckling it. He stared down at Moochie for a minute, watching her reaction to the dope. Once he'd grown tired of watching her, he addressed his goons, "Y'all bring this bitch out to the car, I'll be out there in a second." he told them, pulling out his gun and heading to the bedroom. He pushed open the door of the bedroom with his gun, and walked inside, flipping on the light switch. Seeing a sleeping baby on the bed, he tucked his gun on his waistline and walked over to it. He picked up the baby boy and held him up, staring up into his face. At that moment, he was searching for any resemblance the child may have of him. As far as he could see, the baby didn't look like him or Fonzell. The little dude looked exactly like his mother.

Big Meat cradled the baby in his arms, looking at him as he stared up at him. The baby stretched and yawned, having been awakened from his sleep. The big man scowled at the little dude and pointed his gun in his face.

"You my son, huh? You my lil' nigga? If not, limmie know now, don't be no lying ass bitch like yo' moms." Big Meat continued to hold the gun on the baby, waiting for him to respond. Once the baby shut its eyelids and drifted back to sleep, he tucked his gun back into his waistline. "You know what? It doesn't even matter; I don't want shit

to do with you. I'ma leave you for Fonzell's ass to deal with."

Big Meat carried the baby outside and jumped into his Escalade. As soon as he shut the passenger door, the enormous vehicle drove off in the direction it came from.

****

The Escalade truck swerved recklessly inside of the hospital's parking lot. It nearly knocked the side view mirror off of an oncoming Nissan Sentra heading in its direction. Luckily, it swerved out of the way of the compact car and kept towards the emergency entrance. The SUV halted just outside of the emergency entrance. A moment later, Bumpy and one of the other goons jumped out. They opened the hatch of the big body truck and grabbed Fonzell's ass out of it. He hit the ground hard. They then grabbed him under either arm and dragged his black ass over to the entrance doors, dropping him right outside of them. He lay where he was moaning and squirming, cradling his stump.

"Limmie get the lil' one." Bumpy told Big Meat once he'd knocked on the passenger window and he'd let down the window. The passenger door popped open, and Big Meat passed Bumpy the baby. As soon as Bumpy got him in his arms, he turned around and headed back over to Fonzell. He kneeled down and laid the baby down gently beside Fonzell. His eyes lingered on the child for a moment before he jogged back towards the truck. He jumped back behind the wheel, threw the gear-shift into drive and sped off.

As soon as the truck had left, a nurse ran outside and picked up the baby. She glanced at Fonzell and then called out for help over her shoulder. A couple of mem-

bers of the emergency hospital staff came jogging towards the electric double doors.

"Alright, now it's time you opened the letter..." Fonzell said, staring into the camcorder's lens and waiting for his son to open the letter.

Menace tore open the envelope containing the letter and pulled it out, anxiously. He then unfolded the document and read over it. The line in his forehead deepened the more he read. Shatira was reading right along with him.

"What?" Menace's eyes doubled in size and his mouth hung open.

"Oh, my God!" Shatira gasped, putting her hand over her mouth. Her eyes went big having read the raw and uncut truth. She looked at Menace, and he looked just as shocked as she was.

"I can't believe this! Am I dreaming? Is somebody fucking with me?" Menace asked no one in particular as his teardrops pelted the paternity test results document.

"As hard as it may be for you to believe right now, Big Meat really is your biological father." a teary eyed Fonzell assured him. "I'm sorry that I didn't tell you this sooner. I would have, but I didn't know how to break the news to you."

"Damn, Blood," Menace shook his head, hating to have been hit with the news. "The nigga that's my old head is the same one that set my mom's down the path of self-destruction, and put my pop on ice. Ain't this 'bouta bitch?" he shook his head again, staring down at the document. The teardrops continued to fall from his eyes, so Shatira used the lower half of her shirt to dry his eyes.

"I just want you to know I've always looked at you as my son." Teardrops dripped from the brims of Fonzell's eyes. "I am proud to be your father and have you as my boy. I love you immensely. Peace."

The small screen on the camcorder turned blue and Menace closed it. He then sat it on the bed beside Shatira. She kissed him on the side of his face and threw her arms around him. He stared ahead aimlessly, rubbing his hand up and down her arm. Taking a deep breath, he laid his head against her and shut his eyelids.

Chapter Seven

Shatira took her arms from around Menace and cupped his face in her hands, staring into his eyes. She began kissing him slow and gently, turning her head to the side as they made out. She then pulled away and started biting on his neck softly, causing him to gasp. She slipped her hands underneath his shirt and started playing with his nipples.

"Ba-babe, what're-what're you doing?" Menace asked her with his head tilted back and his mouth trembling. What she was doing was turning him on and causing his dick to nudge at his zipper.

"What do you think I'm doing, huh? What do you think?" Shatira licked up his throat and bit gently along his jawline, as she continued to play with his nipples.

"But I thought you wanted to wait 'til you were married." He licked his lips and gasped again.

"Now or later. It really doesn't matter as long as we tie the knot. You still wanna be my husband, right?"

"Of course I do. As long as you still wanna be my wife." His voice shook as she pleased him, causing his nipples to stiffen.

"Yes. I still wanna be yo' wife." She said as she traced his jawline with the tip of her tongue.

"Then you will in-in a few days. Like-like we planned." He said as his eyelids flickered, enjoying her sucking on his bottom lip.

"Right. But I want this dick now. Are you gonna gimmie my dick now, baby, huh? Are you gonna limmie suck this dick and then fuck the shit outta me?" she asked as she planted a hickie on his neck.

"Y-yes."

"Good. Now, tell me. Tell me to get on my knees and suck this big ol' dick." She said between giving him a hickie and stroking his rock-hard dick.

At that moment, Menace pulled away from her and pulled her back by her hair, looking her in her eyes with hunger twinkling in his pupils. "I want chu to get on yo' knees and suck this dick." He told her with authority, stroking his thick, vein filled dick.

"O-okay, daddy."

"Alright now. Get on yo' fucking knees!" Menace rose from off the bed, pulling his pants down and leaving his dick, curling upward. Shatira hurriedly got down on all fours, like a dog, awaiting the bone that was between his legs. Holding his shirt up with one hand, he walked toward her with his pants around his ankles, bringing his tool near her; its throbbing head oozing with a clear fluid.

Shatira grabbed Menace's dick. As she jacked it up and down it ran with more of the clear fluid, which dripped to the carpeted floor. When she looked up at him, his head was tilted back and he was mouthing something to God she couldn't quite hear. As soon as she put her piping hot, wet mouth on Menace, he stiffen like a dead body and rose to the balls of his red Chuck Taylors. Shatira's head bobbed up and down as she sucked her man off, causing sloshing and slurping sounds to fill the hotel room. Bolts of pleasure shot throughout Menace's lower region. Little momma was blowing him so good that he had to look down at her at work. She was sucking him off with so much passion and intensity that he could have exploded inside of her mouth right then, but he held fast cause he wanted to prolong the pleasure he was getting from her. As Shatira whipped her mouth up and down his shit, he could see ropes and ropes of warm saliva hanging from his shaved nut sack.

"That's right, baby. Suck that dick! Suck that big mothafucka!" Menace egged her on. He then grabbed hold of the back of her head and started jabbing her mouth with his dick, causing her to gag and squint.

"Mmmmmmm! Gag, gag, gag, gag!" Shatira made funny murmuring and gagging noises as she was mouthed fucked. Tears began to build up in her eyes, but she didn't dare stop her man. She wanted to satisfy him in every way sexually. Menace threw his head back and continued to hump Shatira's mouth. When he felt himself about to bust, he popped his dick out of her mouth and grabbed her by her hands, helping her up to her feet. Staring into his face, Shatira wiped her shiny chin off with the back of her hand. She then allowed her man to led her over to the bed.

Menace laid Shatira down on the bed and parted her legs, admiring her bald pussy. He held her breasts firmly and sucked on their areolas, one by one. He then mashed the succulent orbs together and put both of their thick nipples inside of his mouth, sucking on them thirstily. Shatira winced and whined, squirming on her back as her man pleased her sexually. She felt her pussy growing wetter and wetter the longer he feasted on her ample bosom.

"Oh, baby, baby, you doing me so good. Please, don't stop, please, don't." Shatira whined, and then bit down on her bottom lip. Lines creased her forehead and then she bit down on her inner jaw. The small flap of meat nestled between her pussy lips was swollen and throbbing. Menace started groping her breasts as he planted gentle kisses down her torso. She placed her small hands on top of his much larger hands, which were covered with veins. Face balled up, she looked down as he made his way toward her treasure, dying to feel his tongue against her clit.

"Tell me to eat cho pussy, baby." Menace said as he blew his hot breath against her clit, causing her to shiver all over and gasp.

"Eat-eat my pussy, daddy." Shatira obliged his request, licking her lips.

'You want some of this gangsta dick?" he asked, glancing up at her as he continued to blow on her clit.

"Oh, baby, yes, yes, yes." she said, squirming even more now.

"Good. Then, say eat my mothafucking pussy, nigga."

"Okay. Okay, sssssssss." she hissed, anxious to feel his mouth on her. "Eat my mothafucking pussy, nigga!"

With the command given, Menace pressed his tongue against that small flap of meat between her pussy. He started off French kissing it slow and passionately. The way homie was handling her jewel, you would have thought he was kissing her in the mouth. But that wasn't the case. Nah, you see, he was making love to her pussy with his tongue, massaging her breasts the entire time.

"Oh, yes, yes, eat cho, bae! Eat cho mothafucka pussy up, it's yours, daddy. It's all yourrrrrrrrrs!" Shatira cried out as she pushed her head back against the pillow, burying her head halfway into it. She pulled at the sheets, grabbing handfuls of it as her body shook. Lying on the bed, she listened to the slopping and slurping sounds of her man as he devoured her jewel. "Ooooooooh, daddy, what chu doing to me? What's happening to my-my body? Oh, shit, I think I gotta pee, bae! Bae, stop, I gotta pee!" Shatira tried to push Menace's head away so she could get up, but he pinned her wrists to the bed. Head down, Menace started to suck on her clit, causing her eyes to roll to the back of her head and her mouth to tremble. She squeezed her eyelids and bit down on her bottom lip. "Baby, please! I'ma end up peeing on you, please! Ooooooh, fuck, daddy!" Suddenly, Shatira's eyelids snapped open and her back shot up from off the bed. She looked down as she found herself, squirting all in that nigga Menace's mouth. Once she stopped squirting, she fell flat out on the bed, allowing him to lick up her juices.

"That wasn't piss, baby. You were having an orgasm." Menace informed her. He loomed over Shatira stroking himself. Looking at the blissful expression on her face, he tapped his dick against her swollen clit which caused her to whine. He then rubbed his meat up and down it, driving her crazy. He had that ass begging for the dick. "It's time for that dick you asked me for earlier. Tell me you want it, momma." he demanded, wiping the sweat dripping from his brow with the back of his hand. "I-I want it." she rasped out of breath from the intense orgasm.

"Tell me you need it, baby." he stroked his dick against her clit, faster and faster.

"Oh, I need it, daddy. I need it so fucking bad. Give it to me, please." she begged, which caused his dick to get that much harder.

Menace grabbed Shatira by her waist and pulled her closer to him. He then guided his grown man into her pussy. She was snug, but her walls wetness welcomed him in. Feeling her insides made him shut his eyelids and say 'Oh God' under his breath. He couldn't believe how incredibly good she felt.

Menace grabbed Shatira by her ankles and spread her legs apart, creating the letter V. Looking down, he watched his meat slide in and out of her hot, gooey hole.

A devilish smirk spread across his lips as he looked up at the pleased look on her face, as he sped up his stroking of her pussy. She moaned and groaned, eyelids narrowed into slits as she played with herself. As he pumped in and out of her, more and more of her cream lathered up his dick.

"Uh, uh, uh, uh, uh!" Shatira's upper body jumped up and down as her middle was pounded. Menace, who was still holding her ankles apart, stared at her face as he continued to work her center. Beads of sweat formed all over his body and ran down his form, some of which disappeared down the crack of his slightly hairy buttocks.

"Yeah, unh huh." Menace smiled, seeing that he was giving little momma that good wood. "I'm hitting that spot, ain't I? Daddy hitting that spot, baby?"

"Yes, daddy, you hitting that spot! You hitting that spot good!" she assured him.

"That's right! Tell me who pussy is this! Tell daddy who this pussy belong to!" he pounded her harder, causing his sweat to dash onto her hot, damp body.

"Oh, daddy, I'm about to have another orgasm! Oooooh, shiiiiiiit!" her eyelids stretched wide open and her mouth formed an O. Menace was still holding Shatira's ankles and looking down at his dick, jabbing the jewel between her legs, vigorously. She started shaking hard as fuck. Before he knew it, she was squirting all over the stubble of his mound.

Menace continued to dig out that pussy, feeling his dick growing harder and stronger. His nut sack swelled up, and he could tell his dick-head had tripled in size.

"Aaah, fuck, Blood, I'm 'bouta bust! Shiiiiiit, here it come! Here it come!" Menace whipped his glistening dick from out of Shatira. Still holding her right leg, the young gangsta pumped his dick up and down, squirting warm, sticky cum all over her stomach. He continued to pump his meat, squeezing every last drop of his semen out of his pee-hole. He wagged his semi-erect penis, shaking off whatever jizz that was left.

Menace was a little dizzy having come so hard, but he managed to stay up. He hopped out of the bed and walked into the bathroom, grabbing a washcloth. He turned on the dial of the faucet and after a while, hot water flowed freely inside of the bowl. He took the time to get the washcloth wet and soapy. Placing his leg on the toilet lid, he washed her dick and balls real good. Next, he washed out his washcloth and got it wet and soapy again. Right after, he headed back inside of the bedroom, where he cleaned up Shatira's pussy and torso. Once homie was done, he washed the washcloth out with cool water and hung it on the rack.

Menace flipped off the light switch as he walked out of the bathroom. He climbed back into bed and lay on his back. Shatira slithered over to him, lying her head against his chest and throwing her arm across his body. He kissed her on top of her head and caressed her arm, affectionately.

"I love you." Menace told her.

"I love you, too." Shatira replied.

The lovely young couple shut their eyelids and smiled. Shortly thereafter, they drifted off to sleep.

Three days later

Menace and Shatira stood before one another holding hands, with a minister facing them. Shatira was in a beautiful all white bridal gown and Menace was in an all-white tuxedo. The young couple were wearing smiles on their faces. From the looks on their faces you could tell that this was indeed the happiest day of their lives. This was made evident from both of them dropping the occasional tear, taking the time to wipe it every now and then.

Menace and Shatira stared into one another's eyes lovingly, listening to the words of the minister. Once the Man of God said all he had in mind, Menace responded with *'I do'*.

"I now pronounce you man and wife, you may kiss the bride." The minister told Menace and smiled. He watched as the groom lifted the veil that covered the bride's face, sealing their new union with a loving kiss.

There wasn't anyone inside of the chapel after the ceremony, so Menace and Shatira chopped it up with minister for a while before they decided to leave. Hand in hand, the newlyweds walked down the aisle. As they approached the enormous double doors of the holy domain, they saw a African American man sitting in the last pew. He was wearing a hoodie beneath a trench coat. They remembered the man entering the chapel halfway through their wedding ceremony and taking a seat. They figured he was there to have a word with the minister, but when homie suddenly left the chapel they knew that wasn't the case.

"Fuck you think that was about?" A frowned up Menace asked Shatira.

"I don't know, baby. It's probably nothing. Let's not let it ruin our day, okay?" Shatira said.

Menace nodded, and she kissed him sweetly.

Damn, Blood, I shoulda brought my strap with me instead of leaving it in the car. Maybe I'm just studying shit too hard, and our lil' visitor ain't about nothing. Hopefully that's the case.

Menace and Shatira pushed open the double doors of the chapel and the blinding sunlight flooded the holy domain. The loud squealing of the wooden doors startled the pigeons sitting on the porch. The birds flew off in every direction and left feathers floating in the air. Menace and Shatira wore smiles on their faces as they hurried down the steps of the chapel, hand in hand. Once they made it to the sidewalk, they strode toward the vehicle they'd rented for the special occasion, which was a Easter Bunny white Maybach Landaulet. The newlyweds stared into one another's eyes romantically as they walked along. Stopping, they turned to each other and kissed passionately.

Unbeknownst to them, a Dodge Charger was parked across the street from the church they'd just came out of. Its driver's door opened. A man dressed in a duster emerged, wearing a bandana over the lower half of his face and clutching something long, black and deadly. He jogged from across the street in a hurry, glancing in the couple's direction as they continued to kiss. He then glanced up and down the block for any potential witnesses. Confident there wasn't anyone within eye shot of them, he ran faster toward the couple, so much faster that they could hear his boots smacking against the sidewalk.

Shatira was the first one to react when she heard the hard footfalls coming up from behind them. Instinctively, she looked up and locked eyes with the gunman, who'd just lifted his AK-47 up at her. He mad dogged her from behind his bandana and pulled the trigger of his choppa. Menace and Shatira wore shocked expressions on their faces. Menace went to pull Shatira behind him to shield her from gunfire, but she fought him off, shielding him with her own body. Right after, flames were spitting rapidly from the gunman's AK-47. The automatic weapon rattled to life in the shooter's gloved hands, splattering bloody holes in Shatira's upper body. She did a little dance on her feet, and then Menace whipped her around, exposing his back to the gunman.

Blatatatat!

Fire ripped through Menace's lower back and he hollered aloud, falling to the sidewalk on top of Shatira's body. At that moment, the gunman's AK-47 jammed up on him. He turned the choppa to the side and looked down at it. The damn thing was jammed by an empty shell casing.

"Son of a bitch! Not now, I was so fucking close! Fuck!" the gunman bitched and complained as he tried to un-jam the automatic weapon. Once he did, he smiled devilishly and pulled the bandana from the lower half of his face. He then walked upon the bloody young couple as they lay on the sidewalk, his shadow eclipsing them. "Look at me, look up at me now, gotdammit!" Shatira, who was bleeding out of both sides of her mouth and had teary eyes, looked up at the gunman. Menace looked over his shoulder as well. They were both surprised to see Levon staring back at them. "I just wanted you to know who put that work in on you. Now, kiss yo' black asses goodby-"

Ratatatatatatatat!

Bullets ripped through the front of Levon's body, and his blood splattered on the faces of Menace and Shatira. The couple squeezed their eyelids shut as soon as the warm blood splashed them. A wide eyed and surprised Levon whipped around trying to fire his AK, but his shooter walked up on him firing continuously, with an Uzi .9mm. Levon's grill filled with blood and his shoulders danced, as bullets cut his bitch ass in half. He dropped his AK and fell to the ground, not too far from where Menace and Shatira were laying.

Menace looked over at Levon. He was lifeless, staring up at the sky with vacant eyes. Menace was curious as to who the shooter was that saved his life, so he looked up in his savior's direction. It was the same dude that was sitting in the last row of the pews inside of the church while they were saying their vows. He pulled his hood from off his head and revealed his identity. It was his right-hand man and road dawg, Flocka.

"I told you I wouldn't miss yo' weddin', Blood! Oh, shit!" Flocka's eyes grew big once he saw Shatira was lying underneath Menace bleeding to death. "Damn, we gotta get her to a hospi…"

Flocka's words died in his throat when he heard police car sirens heading his way. Right then he panicked, looking back and forth between the bloody couple and his car. He had a decision to make: help Menace and Shatira or make a getaway.

"Go, get outta here," Menace grimaced, feeling the fire in his lower back from getting shot. He knew if Flocka was caught out there with that hot ass Uzi he'd used to lay Levon down, he'd be looking at a lifetime behind bars. That's something he wouldn't wish on his worst enemy.

"Nah, bro, I can't just leave you and lil' momma out here to…"

"No! Go, man, get the fuck outta here, 'fore Twelve show up!" Menace cut him short.

Flocka switched hands with the Uzi. He looked back and forth between the bloody newlyweds and his car, debating heavily. Coming to the conclusion of what he was going to do, and hating it, Flocka swung on the air heatedly and jogged towards his car. He hopped into the driver's seat and tossed his Uzi into the passenger seat. He then fired up his vehicle and busted a U-turn in the middle of the street, going in the opposite direction.

After Flocka had left, Menace focused his attention back on Shatira. She was staring into space with an open bloody mouth. Instantly, Menace's eyes welled up with tears. He shook Shatira gently, and then hard, calling her name.

"Shatira? Shatira? Shatirrraaaa, oh, no! Don't do this to me, baby. Oh, God, I'm begging you, sweetheart! I can't do it. I can't go through this life without chu, baby! Don't leave me! Please, don't leave me!" He broke down sobbing hard, with tears sliding down his cheeks. His head and body shook, as he sobbed long and hard, snot bubbling out of his left nostril.

****

Flocka sped off down the block, punching out, trying to get the fuck out of the area before Twelve showed up. He was just about to cross the intersection when a van screeched to a stop right in front of him. Instantly, the door of the van slid open and a pack of masked up niggaz hopped out, armed with AK-47s with one-hundred round drums. At the forefront of the pack was the tallest of the men. His long hair spilled out from underneath the ski-mask he was wearing and lay upon his shoulders. His menacing eyes peered out of the holes of his mask and peered into those of Flocka's.

"Oh, shit!" Flocka said when he saw all of those motahfuckaz with that artillery. He threw his arm over the shoulders of the passenger seat and looked over his shoulder. He mashed the gas pedal, but hurriedly slammed on the brake pedal. A second van had pulled up behind him, boxing him in. The sliding door of the second van opened and a second pack of masked up niggaz hopped out. These mothafuckaz were armed with AK-47s with them hundred round drums as well. The masked up fools on both ends of Flocka's vehicle, surrounded his car when the tallest of them motioned for them to with his AK-47. The tallest of the gunmen pulled his ski-mask up so Flocka could see his face. It was that nigga, Raffy, the loan shark and bookie. His uni-brow dipped and he smiled wickedly at Flocka. As soon as the young nigga seen him, his heart thudded and his stomach dropped. He already knew what time it was because Raffy's get-down rang throughout the streets.

"You remember me, my friend?" Raffy asked, knowing he had Flocka by the balls and that there wasn't anything his ass could do about it, but accept his fate.

"Yeah, I remember you." Flocka told him. He fished the half smoked blunt from out of the ashtray and sparked that bitch up, blowing out big smoke. He then took a few more puffs, allowing the effects of the gas to put him at ease. "He who fears death," he said, watching as Raffy pulled his ski-mask back down over his face. The Arab and his men then pointed their AKs at Flocka. "Is in denial. Mothafuckaz!" he hollered out at the top of his lungs. Right after, all them niggaz surrounding Flocka's whip sprayed it. Their automatic weapons vibrated in their gloved hands and empty jacketed shell casings danced on the ground at their feet. Fire flickered from out of the barrels of the weapons, blowing hole after hole through Flocka's car. The young nigga threw his head back and squeezed his eyelids shut, gritting his teeth. The bullets riddled his body with holes and splattered his blood on the interior of the vehicle and it's cobwebbed windshield. The broken glass from the windshield fell down into the street, some of it stained with blood.

Raffy threw his hand up and the gunfire ceased. As soon as it did, three police cars sped up on them. The police cars stopped, but before Twelve could step out they were catching hell. Raffy and his niggaz pumped them and their cars full of hot shit. The police cars' windshields shattered, their tires exploded, and the bodies of the automobiles were covered in holes. Raffy and his killaz ceased firing just as a second wave of police cars were pulling up behind them. The police were hopping out of their cars wearing bulletproof vests. Twelve had M-16's and shotguns, and they were taking cover behind their cars. As soon as they had, Raffy and his hittas had finished loading up their spare one-hundred round drums. They whipped around and opened fire. Again their jacketed bullets bursted out windshields, covering the police cars with holes and flattened tires. The police managed to injure some of Raffy's killaz through leg and gut wounds. But majority of the men on their side was getting laid the fuck out. Raffy and them niggaz were firing cop killaz, that's armor piercing bullets. So, their rounds were flying through the police cars and body armor that Twelve was wearing.

"Gahhhhh!" One of the cops hollered out in agony.

Aaaaaah!" Another cop screamed in excruciation.

Raaaahhh!" A third cop shrieked.

Most of them were getting their asses tore the fuck up by those deadly ass cop killa rounds. They fell out in the street. Some of them were still blazing at Raffy and his men, as their comrades pulled them out of the way of the crossfire.

"They're firing armor piercing bullets! You hear me? Armor piercing bullets! We've gotta shoot those bastards in their fucking heads!" the sergeant called out from where he was sitting at the back of one of the police cars. He was holding his bleeding thigh and holding his M-16 up at his shoulder. He looked from left to right as he hollered out his command to his men.

Blatatatatatat!   *Blatatatatatat!*   *Tatatatatatat! Tatatatatatat!*

Live rounds were zipping back and forth. Pieces of car metal and shattered glass was flying, landing in the hair and on the shoulders of police officers as they ducked for cover, trying their best not to get their mothafucking heads blown off. More and more of the police officers succumbed to the fatal fury of the spitting AK-47s, leaving half of a dozen cops fighting for their lives.

After a while, some of the AK firing ceased, as Raffy and his killaz were reloading their automatic weapons. Realizing that it was best to take advantage of the situation, the wounded police sergeant looked to his left and right at the remaining cops. One of them was reloading his M-16 while the other was putting the last of his shells inside the belly of his gauge. Once these cops finished locking and loading their weapons, they exchanged nods with the police sergeant. Afterwards, they swung out from where they were taking cover behind heavily damaged police cars. Swiftly, the cops lifted their firearms and took aim, pulling their triggers. The killaz' head burst like rotten tomatoes hitting the ground. As soon as they fell to their bloody deaths, Raffy and the rest of his hittaz were finishing reloading. The firefight continued until Raffy and a couple wounded cops were the last ones left.

"Aw, fuck!" Raffy said, looking at his mutilated hand. He'd gotten two of his fingers blown clean off. Quickly, he tore off the sleeve of his shirt and wrapped his wounded hand in it, tying it tight with his teeth. When he looked around, he saw all of his comrades lying dead. He scanned the grounds again and saw a couple cops moaning in pain and squirming around. "Fucking pigs!" he snarled and spat on the ground. He then pointed his AK and gave the remaining cops kill-shots, finishing them off.

Blatatatatatatat! Blatatatatatatat! Buratatatatatat!

Movement among the remaining cops ceased. At that moment, Raffy heard a helicopter flying above. When he looked up, he saw a police helicopter. This really pissed him off for some reason. So he ran up on top of the rooftop of one of the police cars and pointed his assault rifle up at it, opening fire. The helicopter flew away unfazed, and Raffy focused his attention back on the street. He realized he was the only living person amongst the exchange earlier. This drove him to laugh maniacally. He started laughing low at first, but then the laughing grew louder and louder. He threw his head back laughing, his stomach jumping up and down.

"I am a God, a God I say." Raffy declared. "A God that walks amongst men! While the rest of you are mortal! Foolish mortals cannot compare to a God! I cannot die! Ever!" he continued laughing maniacally.

Blat!

A bullet ripped through Raffy's forehead, spraying his blood and brain fragments out the back of his skull. His eyes were as wide as saucers and his mouth was stuck open. His neck and legs became as limp as cooked noodles, and he fell awkwardly off the rooftop of the police car, dead.

"Can't die, my ass!" the police sergeant said to no one in particular, slowly lowering his smoking M-16. He'd just put a hot-one through Raffy's dome piece.

"Help, help, someone help us, please!" someone called out from behind the police sergeant. When he turned around, he saw Menace lying on the top of Shatira.

"Hold on, son, I'm gonna radio in for help!" The police sergeant called out to Menace. He then did exactly what he said he was going to do, radio in for help. Afterwards, he scanned his surroundings, taking in all of the bloody dead bodies lying around him. "Jesus," he said, shaking his head, like it was a crying shame. Many of the cops lying on the ground were good friends of his. They were standup men that upheld the law, and went out of their way to help one another. The saddest part about everything was all of the dead cops had families they'd leave behind.

****

"Wake up, baby! Please, wake up! Don't leave me, please don't!" Menace shook and shook Shatira, but she remained still. She was dead. Realizing that the love of his life was long gone, Menace lowered his head and wept into her blood soaked dress. After a while, he lifted his head up and looked up at her face. He swept his hand over her eyelids, closing them forever. He then kissed her tenderly on the lips. Next, he laid his head down on her bosom. Shutting his eyelids, he thought back to the happier times they'd shared.

****

"That day I lost the love of my life. And as a result of being shot in my back, I lost the usage of my legs." A misty eyed Menace said after finishing his story. He was the man that had been chopping it up with Big Meat the entire time. He was Dirty Redd.

Big Meat finished off his double cheeseburger and balled up the paper it came in, dropping it on the ground between his shoes. He then sipped from his fountain drink until he heard the sound that let him know the cup was empty. Afterwards, he took the straw from his lips and belched, shaking the cup to see if the beverage it contained was truly depleted. Discovering that it was, he tossed it aside and smacked the crumbs from his palms.

"You look different, real different, son. I couldn't even tell it was you, especially under that carpet on yo' face," Big Meat grabbed at his chin as he referred to Menace's nappy beard. "I gotta tell you though...knowing that chu hold some sort of animosity towards me, makes me feel uneasy. In fact, I'd probably pop you right now if I was strapped, but then again, look at chu," he looked him up and down, feeling sorry for him being a cripple. "You're stuck in that wheelchair for the rest of your days. You're probably wearing a catheter and a shit-bag just to go to the goddamn bathroom. You can't walk. You for damn sure can't get no pussy with that dead ass dick between yo' legs, either." He shook his head in pity of Menace's condition. "On some real shit, I feel sorry for you, homie, for real, for real. And that's the reason why I'ma spare yo' sorry ass life." Big Meat stood up to his feet and took a good look around him, a jovially expression on his face. There were people coming and going, cars driving past, kids playing around and shit. "Besides, I got bigger fish to fry. You see, my celly was a connected cat. He's about to plug me into some people that's about to have me with some of the best coke money can buy. Once I get that product at my disposal, I'ma be the man again. I'ma bring the 80's back." Big Meat's eyes grew wide and a big ass smile spread across his face. He rubbed his hands together greedily, thinking of all the dead faces he was going to make off the crack game. "Yes sir, the streets gon' love me."

Menace came from under his blanket with a pump action, pistol grip shotgun. He leveled it at Big Meats chest, letting it burst. The first round splattered the big man's chest, dotting the bus stop bench with his blood. Big Meat looked at the big ass hole in his chest, and then back up at Menace. His eyes were as big as saucers and his mouth was hanging wide open. He tried to say something, but two more blast from the shotgun slumped his big ass on the bench. Pedestrians were running back and forth across the street panicky, hoping they didn't catch some hot shit.

"That's for my father, you bitch ass nigga!" Menace tucked the murder weapon back underneath his blanket. He then spun his wheelchair around and rolled around the corner in a hurry. He bent the corner of an alley, where he found a man in a blue cap and matching jumpsuit. He was standing outside of the open shutter of a U-Haul truck which had its ramp extended to the ground.

Menace rolled up the ramp and inside of the U-Haul truck. He turned himself around so that he'd be facing the entrance of the alley. Swiftly, the man in the cap slid the ramp back into its rightful place. He then jumped up onto the metal fender and pulled the shutter down, locking it. He ran around the truck and jumped in behind the wheel, cranking that big bastard up. Afterwards, he switched the gears and mashed the gas pedal, driving from out of the alley. He made his way up a main block, passing several police cars with blaring sirens. A moment later, the man's cellular rang and he answered it.

"'Sup, nephew?" The man spoke into his cell phone.

"We in the clear, Ducey?" Menace inquired.

Ducey twisted his cap to the back. He then looked into the side view mirror and saw that Twelve was way down the street from him.

"Yeah, we straight, man. We in the clear."

"Good." he disconnected the call.

Ducey tossed his cellular into the passenger seat. Next, he cranked up the volume on the radio, bobbing his head as he drove the U-Haul through the streets. A smile was on his face having avenged his best friend, Fonzell's death.

Rest in peace, my nigga. Rest in peace."

The End

Submission Guideline

Submit the first three chapters of your completed manuscript to ldpsubmissions@gmail.com, subject line: Your book's title. The manuscript must be in a .doc file and sent as an attachment. Document should be in Times New Roman, double spaced and in size 12 font. Also, provide your synopsis and full contact information. If sending multiple submissions, they must each be in a separate email.

Have a story but no way to send it electronically? You can still submit to LDP/Ca$h Presents. Send in the first three chapters, written or typed, of your completed manuscript to:

LDP: Submissions Dept
Po Box 870494
Mesquite, Tx 75187

DO NOT send original manuscript. Must be a duplicate.

Provide your synopsis and a cover letter containing your full contact information.

Thanks for considering LDP and Ca$h Presents.

Coming Soon from Lock Down Publications/Ca$h Presents

BOW DOWN TO MY GANGSTA

By **Ca$h**

TORN BETWEEN TWO

By **Coffee**

BLOOD STAINS OF A SHOTTA **III**

By **Jamaica**

STEADY MOBBIN **III**

By **Marcellus Allen**

BLOOD OF A BOSS **V**

By **Askari**

LOYAL TO THE GAME **IV**

LIFE OF SIN II

By **T.J. & Jelissa**

A DOPEBOY'S PRAYER **II**

By **Eddie "Wolf" Lee**

IF LOVING YOU IS WRONG… **III**

LOVE ME EVEN WHEN IT HURTS **II**

By **Jelissa**

TRUE SAVAGE **VI**

By **Chris Green**

BLAST FOR ME **III**

A BRONX TALE

DUFFLE BAG CARTEL

By **Ghost**

ADDICTIED TO THE DRAMA **III**

By **Jamila Mathis**
LIPSTICK KILLAH **III**
WHAT BAD BITCHES DO **III**
KILL ZONE **II**
By **Aryanna**
THE COST OF LOYALTY **II**
By **Kweli**
SHE FELL IN LOVE WITH A REAL ONE **II**
By **Tamara Butler**
LOVE SHOULDN'T HURT **III**
RENEGADE BOYS **III**
By **Meesha**
CORRUPTED BY A GANGSTA **IV**
By **Destiny Skai**
A GANGSTER'S CODE **III**
By **J-Blunt**
KING OF NEW YORK III
By **T.J. Edwards**
GORILLAS IN THE BAY II
De'Kari
THE STREETS ARE CALLING II
Duquie Wilson
KINGPIN KILLAZ III
Hood Rich
STEADY MOBBIN' **III**
Marcellus Allen
SINS OF A HUSTLA II

ASAD
HER MAN, MINE'S TOO **II**
CASH MONEY HOES
Nicole Goosby
TRIGGADALE II
Elijah R. Freeman

<u>**Available Now**</u>
<u>RESTRAINING ORDER **I & II**</u>
By **CA$H & Coffee**
<u>LOVE KNOWS NO BOUNDARIES **I II & III**</u>
By **Coffee**
<u>RAISED AS A GOON I, II, III & IV</u>
<u>BRED BY THE SLUMS I, II, III</u>
<u>BLAST FOR ME I & II</u>
<u>ROTTEN TO THE CORE I III</u>
By **Ghost**
<u>LAY IT DOWN **I & II**</u>
<u>LAST OF A DYING BREED</u>
<u>BLOOD STAINS OF A SHOTTA I & II</u>
By **Jamaica**
<u>LOYAL TO THE GAME</u>
<u>LOYAL TO THE GAME II</u>
<u>LOYAL TO THE GAME III</u>
<u>LIFE OF SIN</u>
By **TJ & Jelissa**

BLOODY COMMAS I & II

SKI MASK CARTEL I II & III

KING OF NEW YORK I II

By **T.J. Edwards**

IF LOVING HIM IS WRONG…I & II

LOVE ME EVEN WHEN IT HURTS

By **Jelissa**

WHEN THE STREETS CLAP BACK I & II III

By **Jibril Williams**

A DISTINGUISHED THUG STOLE MY HEART I II & III

LOVE SHOULDN'T HURT I II

RENEGADE BOYS I & II

By **Meesha**

A GANGSTER'S CODE I & II

By J-Blunt

PUSH IT TO THE LIMIT

By **Bre' Hayes**

BLOOD OF A BOSS **I, II, III & IV**

By **Askari**

THE STREETS BLEED MURDER **I, II & III**

THE HEART OF A GANGSTA I II& III

By **Jerry Jackson**

CUM FOR ME

CUM FOR ME 2

CUM FOR ME 3

CUM FOR ME 4

An **LDP Erotica Collaboration**

BRIDE OF A HUSTLA **I II & II**

THE FETTI GIRLS **I, II& III**

CORRUPTED BY A GANGSTA I, II & III

By **Destiny Skai**

WHEN A GOOD GIRL GOES BAD

By **Adrienne**

A GANGSTER'S REVENGE **I II III & IV**

THE BOSS MAN'S DAUGHTERS

THE BOSS MAN'S DAUGHTERS II

THE BOSSMAN'S DAUGHTERS III

THE BOSSMAN'S DAUGHTERS IV

THE BOSS MAN'S DAUGHTERS **V**

A SAVAGE LOVE **I & II**

BAE BELONGS TO ME

A HUSTLER'S DECEIT I, II

WHAT BAD BITCHES DO I, II

By **Aryanna**

A KINGPIN'S AMBITON

A KINGPIN'S AMBITION **II**

I MURDER FOR THE DOUGH

By **Ambitious**

TRUE SAVAGE

TRUE SAVAGE II

TRUE SAVAGE **III**

TRUE SAVAGE **IV**

TRUE SAVAGE **V**

By **Chris Green**

A DOPEBOY'S PRAYER

By **Eddie "Wolf" Lee**

THE KING CARTEL **I, II & III**

By **Frank Gresham**

THESE NIGGAS AIN'T LOYAL **I, II & III**

By **Nikki Tee**

GANGSTA SHYT **I II &III**

By **CATO**

THE ULTIMATE BETRAYAL

By **Phoenix**

BOSS'N UP **I , II & III**

By **Royal Nicole**

I LOVE YOU TO DEATH

By Destiny J

I RIDE FOR MY HITTA

I STILL RIDE FOR MY HITTA

By **Misty Holt**

LOVE & CHASIN' PAPER

By **Qay Crockett**

TO DIE IN VAIN

SINS OF A HUSTLA

By **ASAD**

BROOKLYN HUSTLAZ

By **Boogsy Morina**

BROOKLYN ON LOCK I & II

By **Sonovia**

GANGSTA CITY

By **Teddy Duke**

A DRUG KING AND HIS DIAMOND I & II III

A DOPEMAN'S RICHES

HER MAN, MINE'S TOO

By Nicole Goosby

TRAPHOUSE KING **I II & III**

KINGPIN KILLAZ

By **Hood Rich**

LIPSTICK KILLAH **I, II**

CRIME OF PASSION I & II

By **Mimi**

STEADY MOBBN' **I, II**

By **Marcellus Allen**

WHO SHOT YA **I, II**

Renta

GORILLAZ IN THE BAY

DE'KARI

TRIGGADALE

Elijah R. Freeman

GOD BLESS THE TRAPPERS I, II, III

THESE SCANDALOUS STREETS I, II, III

FEAR MY GANGSTA I, II, III

THESE STREETS DON'T LOVE NOBODY I, II

Tranay Adams

THE STREETS ARE CALLING

Duquie Wilson

BOOKS BY LDP'S CEO, CA$H

TRUST IN NO MAN

TRUST IN NO MAN 2

TRUST IN NO MAN 3

BONDED BY BLOOD

SHORTY GOT A THUG

THUGS CRY

THUGS CRY 2

THUGS CRY 3

TRUST NO BITCH

TRUST NO BITCH 2

TRUST NO BITCH 3

TIL MY CASKET DROPS

RESTRAINING ORDER

RESTRAINING ORDER 2

IN LOVE WITH A CONVICT

Coming Soon

BONDED BY BLOOD 2

BOW DOWN TO MY GANGSTA

Tranay Adams

CPSIA information can be obtained
at www.ICGtesting.com
Printed in the USA
LVHW040100210319
611370LV00006B/108/P

9 781949 138580